THE CANNIBAL

By the same author

THE BEETLE LEG

THE GOOSE ON THE GRAVE & THE OWL

THE LIME TWIG

SECOND SKIN

THE CANNIBAL

BY JOHN HAWKES

INTRODUCTION BY ALBERT J. GUERARD

A NEW DIRECTIONS PAPERBOOK

FOR SOPHIE

INTRODUCTION

Many introductions exist to persuade the reluctant reader that the classic text under consideration is deservedly a classic, with hidden meanings and beauties. But in the presence of a highly experimental novel, and of such a considerable new talent as that of John Hawkes, an introduction should perhaps attempt no more than to clear away some of the peripheral difficulties and obstacles of strangeness which might prevent an early understanding and enjoyment. No doubt the reader has a right to discover the hidden beauties for himself, during the first years of a novel's life. But isn't it also the novelist's own task, a few readers will certainly argue— "to clear away some of the peripheral difficulties and obstacles of strangeness?" My own answer is that this question can be too costly. The merely secondary difficulties and obstacles involved in the first appearance of a Franz Kafka or a William Faulkner or a Djuna Barnes are not comparable to those involved in the first appearance of a conventional realist . . . and perhaps it would be well if we could get at the restless and original Kafkas at least, if not at the Djuna Barneses, over a shorter period of ridicule, without having to wait so long. I use the names of Kafka and Faulkner and Djuna Barnes advisedly, these august names and coldly intense writers . . . for I think the talent, intention, present accomplishment and ultimate promise of John Hawkes are suggested

by some conjunction of these three disparate names.*
I know that this is to say a great deal, and also to
predict most rashly as to the future direction an
original talent will take. John Hawkes is now, at the
outset of his career and at the age of twenty-three, a
rather more "difficult" writer than Kafka or Faulkner, and fully as difficult a writer as Djuna Barnes.
The Cannibal, written in 1948, is less surrealist than
Charivari, a short novel written in 1947; † and I sus-
pect Hawkes will move still further toward realism.
But his talent, whatever may happen to it, is already
a major talent.

The peripheral difficulties, then, and obstacles of
strangeness . . . The plot is a simple one, but not to
be simply apprehended. There is in the first place
an interesting interlocked story of Germany during
the first world war and of Germany in "1945"—a
mythical year of the allied occupation, when a single
American soldier on a motorcycle is left to supervise
a third of the country. In 1914 Stella, later Madame
Snow, night club singer and daughter of a general,
meets an English traitor Cromwell, and marries the
feeble Ernst. In 1945 Stella Snow's boarding house
in a ruined village harbors her sister Jutta, mistress
of Zizendorf . . . new political Leader and "narrator"
of the story. Zizendorf successfully plots the death
of the lone American overseer and the capture of his
motorcycle; and the book ends with the rebirth of
an independent Germany. For the tiny gutted
Spitzen-on-the-Dein—with its feverish D.Ps., its dis-

* I understand that Mr. Hawkes had all but finished *The
Cannibal* before reading Kafka, Faulkner and Djuna Barnes.
His earlier reading of modern experimental literature was
largely confined to poetry.

† Published in *New Directions 11* anthology.

eased impotent adults and crippled children, with its foul choked canals, with its hunger, militarism, primitive memories and its unregenerate hatred of the conqueror—is Germany itself in microcosm. (As a picture of the real rather than the actual Germany, and of the American occupant of that Germany, *The Cannibal* is as frankly distorted as Kafka's picture of the United States in *Amerika;* and also perhaps as true, thanks to that very distortion.) This interesting story is left very much in the dark, however; is obscured by brilliant detail, by a submersion in many different minds and their obsessions, by a total vision of horror . . . and by a very distinct reluctance (the reluctance of a Conrad or a Faulkner) to tell a story directly. As in Faulkner and Conrad, we have the effect of a solitary flashlight playing back and forth over a dark and cluttered room; the images may be sharp ones, but a casual reference to some major happening may be clarified only fifty or a hundred pages later. The inattentive reader would be hard put to make even such a bare plot-summary as mine; though he might easily go far beyond it—to see in Stella Snow, for instance, both Germany herself and the Teutonic female and fertility principles, the traditional earth-mother of German beer and metaphysics, survivor and protectress of the sterile—"for she had survived and hunted now with the pack."

The peripheral difficulties are obvious enough . . . for the reader who vaguely recognizes his own adult world in *The Cannibal,* as well as his own childhood fears. The story is radically out of focus, which was of course intended; yet there is no consistently distorting point-of-view. The narrator Zizendorf was perhaps intended to supply an even source of distorting light. But Zizendorf, a relative failure, poses more problems than he solves. Again, no character —except Jutta in the single episode of the nunnery— receives that *consistent sympathy* which most of all holds the average reader's attention. John Hawkes clearly belongs, perhaps this to his credit, with the cold immoralists and pure creators who enter sympathetically into all their characters, the saved and the damned alike. Even the saved are absurd, when regarded with a sympathy so demonic: to understand everything is to ridicule everything. And it is also to recognize that even the most contaminate have their dreams of purity which shockingly resemble our own. . . . A third difficulty and distraction is provided, as in Djuna Barnes, by the energy, tension and brilliance of phrasing often expended on the relatively unimportant: the appalling and prolonged description, for instance, of Madame Snow strangling a chicken, a description interrupted momentarily by the appearance of the Kaiser's thin and depressed face at the window.

The final obstacle of strangeness—suggested by the Kaiser's face—is that John Hawkes' surrealism is an independent and not a derivative surrealism . . . I use "surrealism" for want of a better word. There is some traditional symbolism in *The Cannibal;* even perhaps a little old-fashioned allegory. The dead frozen monkey who screams "Dark is life, dark, dark is death"—tail coiled about his neck, "sitting upright on the bodies of the smaller beasts"—is an authentic surrealist monkey. But the ghosts who return each night to the single charred and abandoned allied tank belong to an older literature . . . The basic convention of the novel is this: Germany and the world have shrunk to *Spitzen-on-the-Dein,* rather than the little village enlarged. The characters are passive somnambulistic victims of the divine or diabolic process (history), yet to a degree are aware of their historic position. Thus Ernie running after the carriage of Stella and Cromwell in a German town, stopping in an agony of impatience to relieve himself behind a bush, not merely parallels or suggests but for the moment *is* Gavrilo Princip, the assassin of Sarajevo; and Cromwell and Stella in the pursued carriage prophesy war and offer themselves as historic symbols: "I will become, as you wish, your Archduchess for the people." One could even suggest the peculiarly German conception of a narrator possessed of divine or diabolic omniscience . . . *which the characters enter into or share in occasional moments of intuition.* History is blind, inconsecutive, absurd . . . yet a Stella Snow may foresee it: foresee "the naked cowardice of the fencer, the future fluttering wings of the solitary British plane leaving its token pellet in the market place, her mother's body rolling around it like a stone strained forever, the stain becoming dry and black as onyx."

Of the true solid ingredients of surrealism—illogic, horror, macabre humor—*The Cannibal* has a full share. Terror, for instance, can create its own geography. Gerta almost stumbles over the dead body of the Merchant, on her return from the open latrine, the "pea-green pit of stench," behind the *sportswelt* in *das Grab*. But this merchant, said to have fallen here some months before (page 101) actually fell near Cambrai (page 94), in a farmhouse demolished by artillery fire:

There the Merchant, without thoughts of trade, dressed in grey, still fat, had died on his first day at the front and was wedged, standing up-

right, between two beams, his face knocked
backwards, angry, disturbed. In his open mouth
there rested a large cocoon, protruding and
white, which moved sometimes as if it were
alive. The trousers, dropped about his ankles,
were filled with rust and tufts of hair.

The line between the fantasy of an Edward Lear and
that actual creation of another universe which the
best surrealism attempts is a hard one to draw . . .
the line, shall we say, between two aspects of Col-
eridge's "fancy." Where else do the "monumental
dogs found in the land of the tumbleweed, glorified
for their private melancholy and lazy high song"
belong—unless in the pages of Lear? And yet the
German dogs to which they are compared are fully
as remarkable; and become both real dogs running
beside the train in which the invalided Ernie lies,
and perhaps also recollections of childhood fear; and
some pages later, vague symbols of defeat and death:

Those were certainly dogs that howled. His
face pressed against the glass, he heard the
cantering of their feet, the yelps and panting
that came between the howls. For unlike the
monumental dogs found in the land of the
tumbleweed, glorified for their private melancholy and lazy high song, always seen resting
on their haunches, resting and baying, these
dogs ran with the train, nipped at the tie rods,
snapped at the lantern from the caboose, and
carrying on conversation with the running
wheels, begged to be let into the common parlor.
They would lap a platter of milk or a bone
that appeared dry and scraped to the human
eye without soiling the well-worn corridors of
rug, and under the green light they would not

chew the periodicals or claw the conductor's heels. As paying passengers, they would eat and doze and leap finally back from the unguarded open platforms between cars into the night and the pack.

The temptation to quote from *The Cannibal* is enormous. But no doubt this passage, and the dogs' progressive irresistible taking over of the train and the paragraph, is enough to suggest the author's delight in grotesque distortion—and to suggest the dangers and promises implicit in an imagination so uninhibited and so incorrigibly visual, immediate, obsessed.

How far John Hawkes will go as a writer must obviously depend on how far he consents to impose some page-by-page and chapter-by-chapter consecutive understanding on his astonishing creative energy; on how richly he exploits his ability to achieve truth through distortion; on how well he continues to uncover and use childhood images and fears. Of the larger distortion of *The Cannibal*—of its total reading of life and vision of desolation as terrible as that of Melville's *Encantadas*—there is no need to speak at length. The historic fact of our present effort to reconstruct German pride and nationalism is rather more absurd than the negligent withdrawal pictured by Hawkes. And yet his few "scenes of occupation life" may someday tell us more of the underlying historical truth than the newspapers of 1945 will tell us: the trial and execution of the pastor Miller for having changed his views under the Nazis (the present Mayor betraying him in terror of the curled claws and sharp hooked nose and red terrifying eyes of the eagle on the Colonel's shoulder); the snarling lovemaking of the American overseer Leevey and his diseased German mistress; and the "overseeing" Leevey at work . . . hurtling on his motorcycle through the third of the nation he controls, absorbed in an historical process which transcends any human intention and which he has no hope of understanding. John Hawkes, who saw wartime Germany briefly as a driver for the American Field Service, has written an unpolitical book but not an unhistorical one. As Kafka achieved a truth about his society through perhaps unintentional claustrophobic images and impressions, so Hawkes—abnormally aware of physical disabilities and indignities and degradations—has achieved some truth about his. This is a Germany of men with claws for hands, of women with reddened flesh, of children with braces to support their stumps or their heads. It is a world without food, without hope, without energy . . . reduced for its pleasures to impotent mechanical ruttings bereft of all desire. I think it can be understood that this is more than post-war Germany, whatever the author intended; that this is, to some degree, our modern world. At the end of the novel the liberation of Germany has occurred; or, perhaps, our old world is renewed. This, to be sure, may be looked at in several ways. The insane asylum in *Spitzen-on-the-Dein* is reopened on the next to last page. "At the top of the hill he saw the long lines that were already filing back into the institution, revived already with the public spirit."

ALBERT J. GUERARD

Cambridge, Massachusetts
November 29, 1948

ADDENDUM

Almost fourteen years have passed since the above was written, yet I see no need to revise, erase or retract. There is much more that might have been said. Today, too, I might substitute the term "anti-realism" (vague as it is) for "surrealism" and its often misleading connotations. And of course it would now seem absurd to speak of John Hawkes as "promising." In the years since publication *The Cannibal* never died as so many good first novels do. It kept up its quiet underground life, highly praised from the first by a few, the yellow jacket still present in the serious bookstores where these underground lives occur, the book each year winning new adherents among readers impatient with the clichés and sentimentalities of commercial fiction, or impatient with the loose babblings of the publicized *avant-garde*. *The Cannibal* was reprinted and read.

There was always the possibility Hawkes had exhausted his particular dark vision in this single book, and would write no more. But during these years (while working full time for the Harvard University Press, then as a teacher at Harvard and Brown), he published three more books: *The Beetle Leg* (1951), *The Goose on the Grave & The Owl* (1954, two short novels), and *The Lime Twig* (1961). Each had its different myth and setting, its landscape of an inward geography projected onto a dry impotent American west, onto fascist Italy and San Marino, onto a damp decrepit England of gangsters and gamblers.

The predicted movement toward realism has occurred, but chiefly in the sense that the later novels are much more orderly and more even in pace, and distinctly less difficult to read. The spatial form and dizzying simultaneity of *The Cannibal* are modified. The imaginative strengths remain, however, and the vivifying distortions: the power to exploit waking nightmare and childhood trauma, to summon preconscious anxieties and longings, to symbolize oral fantasies and castration fears—to shadow forth, in a word, our underground selves. And in each of the novels a fine black humor and a nervous beauty of language play against the plot's impulse to imprison us unpleasantly in the nightmare, to implicate us in these crimes. We are indeed deeply involved. But we are outside too, watching the work of art.

Four slender volumes. The achievement may not seem a large one in this day of voluminous and improvising writers, scornful of the right word. Yet it is an achievement roughly comparable in bulk and in variety of interest to that of Nathanael West. Hawkes has of course not written such an easy or public book as *The Day of the Locust;* perhaps he never will. But he has surely exhibited a power of language and an integrity of imaginative vision that West showed very rarely. Hawkes's position is an unusual one: that of the *avant-garde* writer who has imitated no one and who has made no personal gestures of defiance. His defiances—the violence and the indignities and the horror, the queer reversals of sympathy—are all in his books. He has been associated, moreover, with none of the publicized groupings.

Yet for all this lack of politics and compromise, his work appears to be about to prevail. It is being published in France, Germany, Sweden, Italy and England; it has been honored with a National Institute of Arts and Letters award; it has been admired by Cela in Spain as well as by curiously diverse American writers and critics: Flannery O'Connor and Andrew Lytle, Saul Bellow and Bernard Malamud; Paul Engle (one of the first to recognize and praise); Leslie Fiedler, Frederick Hoffmann, Ray West.

The Cannibal itself no longer seems as willful or eccentric as it did in 1948, nor as difficult to read. This is partly in accord with the law that the highly original artist must create the taste that will eventually applaud him. Time, time and powerful reiteration, at last triumph over ridicule. *The Cannibal* prepares us to read *The Lime Twig;* but, even more obviously, *The Lime Twig* and the others prepare us to reread *The Cannibal.* Beyond this, *The Cannibal* doubtless profits from the drift of the novel generally, away from flat reporting and delusive clarities. Readers are no longer as distrustful as they were in 1948 of imaginative distortion and poetic invention, of macabre humor and reversed sympathies, of violence transferred from outer to inner world and from inner to outer. The rich playfulness of Nabokov; the verbal pyrotechnics of Lawrence Durrell and his humorous relishing of decay; the wilder energies of Donleavy and Bellow; the great poetic myth-making of Andrew Lytle and the visions of Flannery O'Connor; the structural experiments of the later Faulkner and the broken-record repetitions of Beckett; and, even, the brilliant ingenious *longueurs* of certain French anti-novels—

all these (to mention only a few of many) show the extent to which the personal and the experimental have been vindicated; have even won public acclaim. Whatever the quickening anti-realist impulse in the novel signifies—whether transformation or annihilation of a *genre* or even a symbolic foretaste of literal annihilation of the self or of matter, a Byzantine decadence or a created myth of dissolution for our time; or whether, more hopefully, a public awakening to new types of fictional pleasure and suasion— whatever all this adds up to helps define *The Cannibal* as a central rather than peripheral work of art and vision.

A.J.G.

Stanford, California
April 14, 1962

THE CANNIBAL

There is a town in Germany today, I cannot say just where, that has, by a great effort, risen above the misery that falls the lot of defeated communities on the continent. It has been slowly bettering itself now, under my guidance, for three years, and I am very nearly satisfied with the progress we have made in civic organization. It is a garden spot: all of our memories are there, and people continually seek it out. But until now there has been only silence for the outside world concerning this place, since I thought it more appropriate to have my people keep their happiness and ideas of courage to themselves.

However, I was forced to leave the town for a short time and while away I made a compromise. For I have told our story. The things that remain to be done weigh heavily on my mind, and all the re-markable activity of these foreign cities cannot distract me. At present, even though I enjoy it here, I am waiting, and at the first opportunity I will, of course, return.

PART ONE—1945

ONE

Beyond the edge of town, past tar-covered poor houses and a low hill bare except for fallen electric poles, was the institution, and it sent its delicate and isolated buildings trembling over the gravel and cinder floor of the valley. From there, one day in the early spring, walking with a tree limb as a cane, came Balamir, walking with a shadow and with a step that was not free, to fall under the eye and hand of Madame Snow. All of Balamir's demented brothers, in like manner, had been turned out to wander far from the gravel paths, to seek anyone who would provide a tin plate or coveted drink. Madame Snow made room for him, setting him at work digging in the basement, in the *bunker,* and the black air closed in about the piles of debris and he was homesick. His feeble brothers were gradually absorbed, whole corps at a time, into the yawning walls, mysteriously into the empty streets and outlying dark shuttered farms, were reluctantly taken off the streets. And yet the population had not grown, the same few brown forms prowled in the evening, the same tatters of wash hung for weeks in the same cold air, and the Census-Taker sprawled, thin and drunk, blue cap lopsided, behind his desk. The town had not grown but the institution had become empty, officials and nurses gone for distant lands, their eyes tight and faces drawn, and over the high narrow buildings no sound could be heard. Every day from the hill, thin

3

children looked down on the empty scorpion that was all that was left of the ordered institution.

A single spire of notched steel hung high above the town, devoid of banners, un-encased by building walls, sticking up above them all in the cold blue evening. Steel rungs hung crookedly exposed all the way up the spire, and steel slabs were driven across the narrow open cellar window where Balamir paused, his white skin wet in the still evening light. Piles of fallen bricks and mortar were pushed into the gutters like mounds of snow, smashed walls disappeared into the darkness, and stretching along the empty streets were rows of empty vendors' carts. Balamir was unprotected from the cold. He found that the wind swept around his wide forehead and parched throat, flew bitterly into the open mouth of his rough upturned stiff collar. He found, in the damp frozen hollow of the cellar, that he could not unearth the wooden bench, the monstrous curling vase, the moldy bureau, or any of the frozen pots in uneven jumbled piles, littering the earthen floor and reaching to the rafters. He found that the earthen padded walls muffled his long howls at night and left the sound only in his own ears. While he worked, picking with the coal shovel, or sat staring up at the window, paper-wrapped feet shuffled overhead, and in the inhabited kitchens of the town the candles flickered, cans of thin soup warmed over flickering coals, and the children whined. Bookstores and chemist's shops were smashed and pages from open books beat back and forth in the wind, while from split sides of decorated paper boxes a shoft cheap powder was blown along the streets like fine snow. Papier-mâché candies were trampled underfoot. In outlying districts, in groups of four and five, Balamir's brothers chased over the rutted and frozen ground after the livestock, angry and cold, their thick arms wagging, or clustered around the weak fires, laughing and cold. A small number of these men, after flinging hatchets or raging momentarily in the dark with stained knives, walked back and forth in the cells of the town jail, beating themselves and damning incoherently. The rest, including Balamir, did not realize that they were beyond the institution's high walls. The population of the town remained the same and thieves from the jail went home to keep the balance.

Madame Snow, owner of the building, living on the street floor above the cellar room, would have been a grandmother had not her son's child died, no bigger than a bird, in an explosion not a block away. In the still morning air, the frosted fields about the town had cracked with the infrequent thudding of small explosions, and those that had discharged in the town had left a short useless whistle in her ears. But the children of Madame Snow's sister had survived, to crawl sexless and frightened about bare rooms. Time after time, for months before Balamir had come, Madame Snow had watched the thin men climbing down from boiling trucks, waiting to see her son's return. When he had finally arrived with his stump and steel canes, with special steel loops circling up about his wrists for extra support, he had not added even one bare number to the scratched-out roster of the drunken Census-Taker. He had returned to his wife and rooms in a corner of the moving picture house, and from then on, worked with the black machine in the hot projection room, showing each day the same blurred picture to no audience. Madame Snow did not see him after that.

She busied herself as janitor, arguing with the residents or giving comfort; or sat in the large gilt chair tying rags together and infrequently pulling the heads from small fowl. The halls no longer smelled of roasting swine or boiling cabbages, no longer rang full with heavy laughter, but remained dark and cold, streaked with mud from the roomers' boots.

The building slanted crookedly and silent in a row of black stained fronts and the canal drained past the back fence; on the corner where the side street met the empty thoroughfare was the rising jumble of the steel spire. When a boy with black peaked martial cap, leather braces and short trousers walked past the drawn curtains, Madame Snow would peer hungrily out and then go back to the darkness. On the third floor of the house was the apartment of the Census-Taker, who left his dripping cape flung in the downstairs hall. Herr Stintz, a one-eyed school teacher, lived on the fourth floor, and above him, with her children and bleached plants, lived Jutta, the sister of Madame Snow. Herr Stintz, ex-member of the band, played his tuba late into the night, and the notes fell on the cobblestones recalling the sound of fat marching feet. But the roomer who lived on the second floor was out.

"Come," said Madame Snow to Balamir, "come in. The room gives no heat really, but off with your coat. You're at home." Balamir knew he was not at home. He looked at the small table with the rows of playing cards and single gilt chair, looked at the bright figures where Madame Snow played alone. He carefully looked about the room of court and puzzled about the oaken whorls above the curtained door and the highness of the spidery black ceiling. "Sit down," said Madame Snow, afraid to touch

6

his arm, "sit down, please." But he would not. He would never sit when anyone could see him. So he stood in the middle of the floor and a dwarfed cat rubbed against his leg. The attendant, hat pulled over his face and rubbers thick and too large, gave a sheaf of worn papers to Madame Snow and left like a shadow.

"Will you drink tea?" He looked into his hands, saw steaming water and watched a single star-shaped leaf turning slowly around near the bottom of the cup. He saw a pale color slowly spread, creeping up the china towards his fingers, watched the star turn and the cup dip like the moon. But he would not drink. The little woman watched him from the side of her eye, the light almost gone. His hair was rough and shaggy and he would not drink her tea. Down in the cellar Balamir put the coat on again, standing until she hurried back up the stone steps, for he could feel the cold. "Good night," she said and turned the brass key.

Jutta's child, shoes undone and lips white, ran along a path through the rubble, stumbled over stones, passed overhanging iron ledges and shattered windows, tried to weep, and fled on. A man followed, swinging a cane, craning into the darkness. The child passed a wall spattered with holes and the fingers of a dead defender, and behind him, the man coughed.

A butcher shop was closing and a few cold strands of flesh hung unsold from hooks, the plucked skin and crawling veins uninspected, hanging, but without official sanction. Wire caught the child's knee.

The town, roosting on charred earth, no longer ancient, the legs and head lopped from its only horse statue, gorged itself on straggling beggars and remained gaunt beneath an evil cloaked moon. Rattling trains turned back at the sight of the curling rails blossoming in the raw spring on the edge of town opposite the hill, and fields, plummeted with cannon balls, grew stained with the solitary need of beasts and men. As the old families returned to scrub again on the banks of the canal or walk singly dressed in black, the prisoners filed out over the hills, either as names on a ticket, or if the ticket had been lost, simply as uncounted numbers. When an old man was gripped dying in a terrible cough, Jutta was betraying her lost husband and bearing child again. The town, without its walls and barricades, though still a camp-site of a thousand years, was as shriveled in structure and as decomposed as an ox tongue black with ants.

The Signalman, girded with a blanket in a wicker chair, smoking a pipe like a porridge bowl, commanding the railway station and a view of empty benches, no longer raised the red arm or pulled down the yellow, and no more lights blinked before his fat eyes to disturb his memories of the war of 1914. He had nothing to eat and nothing to say, and black men in large hats and capes were painted all over the walls of his station. Relics of silver daggers were looted from the nunnery and stored in trunks with photographs, or taken off to foreign lands. The bells never rang out. Fires burning along the curbs and dung heaps smoldering on the farms filled the air and alleys, the empty shops and larders with a pungent smell of mold.

The Mayor, with his faded red sash, was too blind to tend the chronicles of history, and went hungry like the rest with memory obliterated from his doorstep. Their powerful horses of bony Belgian stock, dull-eyed monsters of old force, had been commandeered from the acre farms for ammunition trucks, and all were gone but one grey beast who cropped up and down the stone streets, unowned, nuzzling the gutters. He frightened the Mayor on black nights and trampled, unshod, in the bare garden, growing thinner each day, and more wild. Children took rides on the horse's tail and roamed in small bands, wearing pasteboard Teutonic helmets, over the small confines of the town, their faces scratched and nails long. The undertaker had no more fluid for his corpses; the town nurse grew old and fat on no food at all. By mistake, some drank from poisoned wells. Banners were in the mud, no scrolls of figured words flowed from the linotype, and the voice of the town at night sounded weakly only from Herr Stintz's tuba. Bucketfuls of sand kicked up by minor grey duds had splattered against flaking walls and trickled onto worn doorsteps where chickens left frightened tracks. Rotting sandbags killed the weeds, filled the air with the must of burlap, and when they fell to nothing, left white blotches over the ground.

The townspeople had watched the bands of men march off and later come back with venereal diseases or their ears chopped from their skulls. One night startled eyes watched the coat of arms on the castle wall go up in smoke and flame as if an omen that they were expected to rally round for their sons or weep bitter tears. The Mayor lost at cards, had witnessed executions with his eyes closed, and in the marrow of his thick bones, the town shrank. All bartering was done by hand, the flowing script was chipped from the fat walls of the bank and the barred windows of the institution grew dense with cobwebs. An overturned tank on the north road still crawled with ghosts who left it at night and hung over the canal walls for drink.

The Signalman, his mouth clamped shut, sitting behind the postered window of the station, saw the boy dashing over the torn rails and saw the man with the cane coming behind, his shadow lengthening in the station's candle light. Jutta waited with her hungry little girl bouncing up and down, riding her knee. The damp smell of the river rolled over soldiers' leggings and trousers that had been left in doorways, and a cow lying dead in a field looked like marble. In the tenuous light of day, Madame Snow hunched over her cards, and the silver platters, goblets and huge bowls grew black with tarnish and thick with dust. The merciless light showed each house a clear red or flat sand color and long burned beams and ashen barns were black. The green of cabbages had turned to white, and small automobiles, stalled and punctured to the side of the road, were blood red. Everyone wore grey, and over their shoulders were hitched empty cartridge belts. They begged while queuing for food and pounded their foreheads with their fists.

Throughout these winters Madame Snow could not believe that the worst would come. All her faith was in the knuckle bones of a worthless currency, in the right of the victorious, a coinage covered with the heads of high-spirited men. Bits of gauze were pushed into the clay and women wore coats with epaulettes and brass buttons. In the early days when the patients had rioted at the institution, it was the women who beat them down with clubs, while girls with spirited eyes and bare knees lured officers to a night of round-the-world. Arms and armies and silver blades were gone, the black had come out of the realm of kings, and butterflies and grass were left for children. Freight trains were hit and burned and no more came, and the keys of all machines were welded together. *Wohin gehen Sie?* cried the devils, and the clatter of boots died out of the barracks.

Balamir came eventually to think of himself as Madame Snow's Prince. But for a long while he worked by himself, still smelling drugs and fighting with the terrible shapes that leaped from drawers. He longed to be in the mountains, to leap from crag to crag, fly about the snow fields and find gold at the foot of stunted trees. He longed to tend the sheep and be a gangling black dog racing at the herd over green slopes. He longed to live in a cave. Icicles hung between the slats of the cellar window at night, and Balamir began to think of the jewels hanging from the ears of Madame Snow, began to listen for the turning of the key. He listened for the only accordion in the town and the notes traveled down the rain pipe, over the slate, but no voices sang to the crashing of the steins. There was nowhere to eat in *Spitzen-on-the-Dein,* and tables were piled on one another, chipped with bullet-holes. Sometimes Balamir heard sleigh bells that jingled in the valleys of the Alps, and he flung himself on piles of cold rubbish and earth as on a snow heap. He slept on an army cot, longed for the fir trees, and as he grunted and threw his weight every day into the frozen articles of chairs, springs and picture frames, he felt that his strength was falling away. He remembered photographs of the vicious tigers and the days when all men wore spats or silver braid, and from the mountains to the *Brauhaus,* camps and meeting halls sprang up, precision glasses were trained. He thought of a pigtailed donkey and the bones of men ground

11

into food. But now the guardhouse was empty, his father, who had been the Kaiser, was dead, and the nurses had been taken from the institution as corporals. He began to sit at the top of the stairs waiting for the door to open.

Madame Snow, Stella Snow in the days of laced boots, parasols and Grand Balls, had loved white prancing horses, square-shouldered men with spikes rising from their helmets, and sleek sausages that bulged like pig's hind legs, hanging in the kitchen large as a palace. She had breasts for a young girl, and had sat many times in a golden opera box, her legs growing rigid as if she were posing for a picture. The food in her father's house was served encased in layers of fat and from a basket at the side of her bed she had eaten a hybrid kind of giant pear. She went out with young men dressed in black who could ride a horse up to the point of death on a winter's day and leave him to freeze, feeling the hand of hell's angel, or went with moustached students with orange bands about their caps. She craved candies imported from France and Holland, heard lovers sing in raucous voices, and punting, seemed the image of the passing swan. She had a mouth that inverts envied, and when the first thuds of cannonade rocked the country, the mouth closed and she began to read. She loomed like a waxen noncommittal saint when her mother fell before her in the street from marketing, a piece of metal jutting from the bosom, while the airplane crashed. The policeman blew his whistle and people ran from every hole, looming like roaches before her startled eyes. It was then that she imagined marble bannisters and the candelabra of several generations before, and saw strange men embarking in ice-covered ships. Machine guns slowly rattled in the raked forests. Her sister, young and sullen, tore pages from books and leaped in the snow. Stella took to cards, gambling, to singing, and finally back to cards, and in the meantime crossed barbaric swords hung over her head and she swept through ironclad centuries, a respected crone.

Doors clamped shut and single lamps were lit. Jutta fondled the unformed girl while her son, awkward as a doll, ran over the cold earth. Many boys had been crushed under the tread of monsters and there were no martial drums to roll, though women pulled up their skirts to catch the tears. The shadows about the child seemed like beasts of the circus, groaning out of the empty doorways with nothing to mangle in their jaws. About him the wind began to scream as through the slots of airplane wings. The child ran, but only a sharp eye would have told that he was a boy, for his face, hands and hair were as flat as his sister's, and the light from his eyes was as limpid and sullen as the night. Still, the Duke hooked his cane over his arm, adjusted his suede gloves, and followed, his trouser cuffs becoming wet with mud. The child ran all the faster when the light went out of the butcher shop.

The shutters on the Mayor's house were closed as they had been ever since the time of air raids. The collar of his nightshirt was dirty and torn and he pulled the covers over his head. He smelled damp wood, the stone, goose feathers. And when he heard the footsteps running in the street below he shivered; for as a Hun, only *he* knew responsibility and the meaning of a coat of arms, the terror of a people left without tribunal and with privation. The Duke walked past the Mayor's house, unafraid of a hand in the dark, whistling softly to himself, but his eyes were sharp and he was keen on the scent. Then out of the blackness came a man, fresh from an alley, his hands still wet, breath strong with spirits. He reeled and they bumped below the Mayor's bedroom window. It was the drunken Census-Taker. He stepped back, looked up at the tall figure. "Ah, Herr Duke," he said, and his eyes searched the face. "You are mistaken," said the Duke and pushed on.

There was no sound. It was years since the people had stopped talking, except for fragments of a sentence, "Madame Snow told me to die . . ." And these words were only uttered in the strictest of confidence and in the lowest voice, for they had all the same experience, yet expected an alien ear, waited for disbelieving eyes. Even when the butcher shop door slammed shut, it seemed to say, "Quiet. I am not really closed." "Believe only in ten Gods," most people said. "For Evil is a punctual being; our mothers and fathers founded the State; our prisons have since become empty; the Crown must pass from hand to hand; and Stintz is a good devil with our children. Our money will not burn forever; even the sow's hoof is armed; one of our devils is just the time of day. We recall the rites of Wittenberg, and our tempestuous wives beat the fair young girls." When they spoke of the darkness of the weather, or of the lack of clothes, they were referring to one of the ten Gods of Loss whom they could not trust. And when they spoke their lips hardly moved and they were unable to believe their own words, expecting some agent to rise out of the middle of the table and condemn or laugh. Of Nordic stock, they were silent, the tribal cry long dead from their rolling tongues.

14

The Census-Taker moved away, drunken but conscious, fearing to make a sound. His belt sagged round his waist, his eyes rolled as with columns of figures. In the back of his mind he turned over a hatred for the Mayor, who had witnessed executions with his eyes closed. Pulling his cap more over his ears, he knocked softly on the door of the *Crooked Zeitung,* the town newspaper. At the end of every evening he stopped at the Paper, and it was then that his heart grew bright and the old excitement returned. Each letter in the plates of type was butchered into the next, all the plates had been smashed with hammers, and throughout the office was the smell of gum and the half-light from broken eye shades. The roll-top desks were smashed open and mice crawled over the bottles piled in the corners.

Jutta's husband had owned the Paper, but he was lost among thousands in Siberia, and I, Zizendorf, his friend, sat through every hour of the day thinking of the past. I too awaited this hour after midnight when my visitor would come, when I could cease thinking of lines of inverted print, and of the spoils I had found but had never seen again in Paris. I alone was editor, but my fingers were too blunt to punch the keys and I had no paper.

"Good evening, Editor," said the Census-Taker, "and how are you tonight?"

"Sit down for a moment," I said.

We always talked for an hour, then left together. We drank together and our pale eyes took in the cobwebs and then we would think of songs now unsingable. But we knew that there was something to do after our few words. We could talk of nothing and yet there were smiles hidden under our faces. We adjusted our clothes, drank slowly and carefully,

15

both knowing we would leave when the time was right.

"Well, we still have no government," I said. My eyes looked over the steel glasses.

"My friend, I can only think of plenty tonight. I remember festive costumes and bright lights. But you are right, we have nothing."

We both smiled, legs stretched limply before us, smoke rising from saved cigarettes. The kerosene burned low and problems were as flimsy as its slight flames. We heard our own breathing. I sometimes thought of Jutta's husband, who had been a good fellow, of spring and beerhalls, but more often I thought of the Pastor I had shot to death, of perfumes and earrings, and the keys that would not work, words that would not come. We heard the distant sound of the low water in the canal, felt our hunger growing stronger. The shadows grew larger in the printing office. "Shall we go?" asked the Census-Taker. He could feel the warmth creeping upon him. I strapped the pistol under my arm, blew out the lamp, and we left.

Jutta's girl was named Selvaggia and she was like a small white statue when she was undressed. Her widespread eyes were always afraid, even though the only person she feared in all the world was Herr Stintz. That man, one floor below, was playing a dirge on his tuba, his shiny head reflected from its bell, the sounds falling chromatically down and down. The mother held her child at arm's length, and the child seemed to grow like the pit of a fruit from the dotted kimono sleeves, straddled, as if she could never fall, on the woman's knee. The mother was starved for food, a woman who had gorged herself on nuts, cream, shanks of meat and chocolate, but now filled herself at night in a way that her daughter, or son, could not. Her head belonged to a man, but though the face was male, her breast was still a woman's. The flat couch filled almost all the room and became her larder. Jutta was like her father, a Prussian mouth, a Roman nose, strong legs now, years after her illness, but her daughter was unlike any of them, a child on a poster. Stella Snow resented Selvaggia and her brother for bearing no resemblance to the family, and they would not speak to her. Jutta hated Stella from the first day her small man's face looked up from the crib to see her older sister staring down, mouth too filled with tongue to speak. The candle flickered and Jutta and child heard the double pairs of boots on the stairs, heard the sound clumping up like drummers' flams out of the silence. Selvaggia ran off to the second room to wait alone for her brother. She was wide-awake. She heard the opening of the door, the words *"Guten Abend,"* then shut them all out of her mind. In the next room the three of us lay on the couch.

Madame Stella Snow combed her half-white, half-gold hair, hung her black gown from a hook on the wall and crawled into the bed. A resident of the town for twenty years, knowing them all more closely than the Mayor, she felt the pain more acutely than he, even with her heart more like stone. Even though there was no Post, even though no one came or went and they all had lived or died for many centuries, even though there was no wireless, she felt the vastness of community that was like burial, spreading over all borders and from family to family. No drainpipes, chemicals to cleanse, flames to heat, no word, no food for the young or old, she was puzzled. Despite her years she could not find where

17

it had all begun, for she was aristocratic to the end. Stella was capable of anything with a cold heart, but she could not bear the mutilation of any part of her. So she would not see her son. Distorted trees and rattling windows, dirty uniforms and an individuality that meant death flowed in a dangerous stream through *das Grab*. Even she, feeling the hunger, sometimes hesitated bringing the goblet to her lips. She had spent an oddly sexual decade and was now more unlike her sister than ever. Limbs of trees scraped against the window; she remembered that her sister's boy was still out in the night. She lay in the dark. Then she heard the scratching at the cellar door.

All Germany revolved around Balamir. His feet were in the boots of an Emperor's son, he felt the silver sword of time and tide and strength against his hip. Growing weak and cold, he was the result of commands coming down out of the years. From the farm where he was born to the institution and munition works, he felt that people bowed as he passed. How he sought to be that image, how the Kaiser's ghost needed him, how he would be Honor in the land he had become. But how well he knew it was a reign of terror and felt like pulling his beard as his father would have done. Potentate of the north, he scowled on his subjects, the trees, the chips of broken glass, brass casings and beaten fuse ends, but alone he smiled on his castle walls. He was the true and unknown Prince of *Spitzen-on-the-Dein,* followed by the castrated and the disillusioned, guided by an unknown hand around the signs of the skull and cross-bones planted above the mines. He had crept about the door of the Duke's apartment, watched the tall man come and go. He used to walk in the institution's garden, and now, in the last days of the decline of his kingdom, he was befriended in the home of twittering birds.

The vapors of the canal grew stronger, the Duke gained a hundred feet and eased his pace, cracks and holes in the earth filled with night dew.

I unstrapped my pistol and put it on the floor.

More insistently Balamir's fingers scratched at the door, and hunched on the top step he thought of a balcony and an armored knight. Germany lay below in the darkness.

"Come in, you poor creature," she whispered, and the trenches of the countryside were suddenly seen by the light of her candle.

TWO

To countenance the sickle over the wheat, to sweep out of the years the mellow heartbreak or the grand lie, to strike forward barehanded to a very particular and cold future, a diminutive but exact ending, a final satisfactory faith that is cruel and demonic, is to suffer the highest affection and lose it, to meet the loss of life and the advent of a certain reality. Madame Snow, having once reached the full period of life with her husband Ernst, and having fallen, alone, from such a richness, had met and lingered on this exact desolate end. Whereas Jutta, kin in place only, having spent a barren rigid past, was just now reaching the turn in the road where nakedness seemed to hang like a hundred apples, pink, wet, and running with sweet stiff worms, and she would probably never in her own time recognize the life-less segments of Germany threaded on a string before an open window. She indulged herself where her sister Stella had entered with daring.

The Census-Taker, stretched full length on the flat of his back, attuned to every breath over the bed and with his soul dissociated from the actual room, felt a persistent gentle quiver through the sheets, a rippling noise from the most infantile spaces. The curtains that hung over the window, not around it, the covers that hung from the foot of the couch, were not at all princely, but were washed clean and sparse. They were passed over many counters, spun from an ordinary thread. He had no heart for rebellion, still wearing the blue cap of an official crushed under one ear, had no ability to desire or to crush the tingling noise or presumptuous motion. While Jutta and I needed, in a skinned momentary manner, this vague ordeal, he was only able to absorb some faintly gross misunderstanding of already abnormal passions, some slight frightening tendency toward reversion, darkness and pleasure. The single globe overhead, burning at the end of a current without direction, diffused a light through the wings of moths, yellow, soft—a reality clear enough to see. The floor was swept clean for the children. Jutta did not seem to know of the Census-Taker's presence, did not feel his cold shoes against her bare feet, or the rough stubble on the back of his hands, but moving in an artifice, a play she well knew, pursed her lips into an act, an act to rid herself.

No one could dislike Jutta, though she was as nervously strong in her adult years as Stella was in her turning girlhood; she was as kind as a maternal spirit with a patriarchal plain nature, and whatever wisdom she may have felt lay restless, lost beneath the sheets. To me she lay in beauty, and into the Census-Taker she breathed a tense laughter, still trying to complete in her middle year some joyless cycle. And to the others, the cold white ravenous men and trunks of women, without age, without passion, she was the younger sister of Madame Snow, half-warm, half-friendly. She persisted in believing that both her children were her own, could not admit their creation with any man, and believed that they both loved her with the clarity of children who have not yet reached the size of youth. She breathed closer into my ear, traced the smooth canals, followed those old repeating dreams and murmured words. I was a counterfeit, a transformer for several delicate whims and exasperating needs, was an image for the moment made from past respectable devices. I rolled up on my side as if awake, and I saw in her body something that was not there, something that graced, I thought, the nibbling lips of the goat.

The Census-Taker, feeling the unnoticeable height of his own small passion, moving with stealth and awe as a child before the hanging sock, moving as if he held it in his hands and would not fracture it, slid from the bed and walked tiptoe to the corner chair, hung for a second, then turned to see. The most sensitive pulsations trembled at the corners of his eyes, and leaning slightly forward, verdant under the yellow light, he watched. His pleasure broke for a moment remembering a week the Americans had occupied the town and he had been forced to watch, deadly drunk, eyes red, while the Mayor, wretched and awkward, looked the other way and dropped the handkerchief that ended Pastor Miller's life at the stake. He concentrated and the steady movement returned, broken with the intricate strokes of pleasure. His memories were not as frequent or particular as my own. But I, Zizendorf, had now forgotten all under my undramatic and specialized dark guise, and I looked into the white of the sheets.

"What are you doing?"

"Why, I don't remember. Does it matter?"

"No."

A haunch rose above the white, then receded like an iceberg drawn just below the surface, the springs making hardly any noise, interest waiting for the chance to disappear. Night after night we waited for this summoning of flagged energy, hands cold, eyes closed, while in other beds and lofts the sleepers could not awake, could not breathe. My need to recreate, with amazing frequency, some sort of pastime similar to my comrades' habits, a cyclic affection that had finally, in Paris, become fatal to their health, led me to the quite real bargain of Jutta on the top floor. I, the Editor, did not recognize the head in the hay or fathom the posed deep slumber of the houses I passed on my nightly journey. And somehow the Census-Taker was my relic-brother, whose actions and despairs, whose humorous awkward positions and dry attempts were similar to mine. The Census-Taker, who had stature only through responsibilities that had gone, was muddled and lopsided as the badge of his marine cap, was unable to count or to repeat the names. He sought the appearance of love in the lives of his friends, retaining out of his official experience a disgust only of death. He lived the smallest chip of illusion, bearing along his drunk path a recognition of the way, a small dropsy formula that might in the end lead him out, beyond the overt sorrow of his partially thrilled, sitting figure.

My first days in Paris had been difficult. "Dear Sister," I wrote, "I'm having a bad time and cannot seem to get started in enjoying myself. I find the women very hard to get—the release here has broken down all our official routine and rank, and in consequence I do not seem to have anything with which to gain their respect . . ." Now with Jutta it was different, more like the second part of my Paris trip when I'd somehow found my nerve and hence perfume and boudoir parties. I enjoyed the Census-Taker watching us from the chair.

A low repressed rumble from the cold radiator

sounded like the beating of crickets' wings, his increased breathing slowly died down while our activity on the bed at his feet remained at a constant low level, consistent and unvaried without end. Gradually he sank back in the chair, his knees spread, belt pulled in, while he brushed with one hand at the image of Miller.

The Duke, shortening the pace, picked his way carefully by the cliff of fallen walls and poked with his cane into the dark crevices, hoping to stick the crouched body of his prey, to light upon the thin fox. He came legitimately by his title, and when he had commanded three tanks in the second war, was known as a fearless man. A father much older than himself still stalked far away in Berlin where I had never been, and as his father would have done, he recognized with taste and profound respect the clear high and stable character of Madame Snow. The night was so black that the red lights from the hatches of his tanks would have reflected against the clouds and brought death. Free of the debris he again approached in the path of the child, not quite able to visualize the kill.

Jutta did not know the Duke, did not like him, and immediate instinct told her to beware the second floor, for she feared his clean standing, feared his aristocratic caliber which she, through her own fault, had not grasped from her family. She spoke of most intimate life with her daughter, tried to instill in her son ideas of manhood, and spent a certain part of the day sweeping dust into a little bin and rubbing with a damp cloth. She left her apartment very seldom, but even the Duke, in his most precise manner, had noticed her gentle convolvulaceous long legs. Large and perfect in every detail but not a woman, sensible and sometimes calm but not a man, she failed to understand the German life, failed as a mother, at least for her son. She had never been quite able to allow a love for her country to intrude within her four walls, had never been loyal, and though she gave herself like segments of a fruit, she never envisioned the loyalty due her State. Tears sometimes appeared on her cheeks after our long embrace which I was never able to recognize. Thirty years is not enough time to measure the complete crystallization of a nation, though partially lost; to measure the greatest advance of communal men, though partially destroyed, and Jutta, far removed from the rise, fall, and eventual rise, was far from being within the thirty years, far from being successful or adored.

"Again?" She spoke under my arm. "Perhaps you are right. You certainly are, here . . ." There was hardly a break as the wheel turned, sustaining the light ardor. No movement could be carried long enough to last over to the first minute after, beneath the yellow globe.

Tonight she seemed lovely, now propped against the pillows, resting a knee against my side, her eyes passing once over the sleeping Census-Taker, then towards the door of the other room, robe-top arrested and wrinkled below her waist, lovely, but far from the majesty of Madame Snow, who looked very old. She was never able to tell when I would come, but at a moment she would find me. Now she relaxed while I touched her arm with the flat of my cheek.

Yesterday she had gone for a walk, down the steep loose stairs of the boarding house, grey shawl over the bent shoulders, bringing with love and kindness her daughter Selvaggia, who followed behind. She reached back for the long hand to guide the child in the darkness, pushed open the door with her foot, and outside they found that the town was partially destroyed, that a cold spring sun was cut through by a rough steel shoulder, that cold ruts of mud were beginning to thaw. Her face had no color under the sunlight, mother and daughter walked in the same slow stride, feeling their way forward in a place they did not know, and the child spoke now and then in a friendly way. Jutta drew the shawl closer, tried to keep her black shoes free of the mud.

"What were the invaders like?" asked Selvaggia.

"They were bad people, but they didn't stay long." The child had been protected from their sight the week that the Americans had stopped in the town; now they had scurried on to the further cities, and only a man on a motorcycle came occasionally to *Spitzen-on-the-Dein*. His saddlebags were full and his handsome machine roared across untraveled roads with authority. But his face was covered with goggles and Selvaggia had only seen him bouncing quickly, noisily, through the streets.

"You shouldn't even think about them," said Jutta, and she vaguely hoped that her child would not.

In the sunlight Jutta's hair was not so pretty, pin-head eyelets of dirt were on her nose, spots in the loose dress had run, her legs were large and stiff under the re-stitched swinging hem. Her daughter's face narrowed to a thin point at the chin and it seemed likely that the child would never have breasts. Under the narrow fish-bone chest where they might have been, her heart beat autonomously, unaffected by the sight of the hill of sliding moist

Sonoma County Library

**This item is due on the month
and day punched out below.**

JAN	FEB	MAR	APR	MAY	JU●
JUL	AUG	SEP	OCT	NOV	DEC

1	2	3	4	5	6
7	8	9	10	11	12
13	14	15	16	17	18
●	20	21	22	23	24
25	26	27	28	29	30
31					

Fines are 20¢ a day on general items and
10¢ a day on juvenile items.
Fine for videos is $2.00 per day.

clay. The tar-paper houses on top of the hill were sunken at the ends, jewels of tin cans littered the indefinable yards without lawns or bushes, and hostile eyes watched mother and daughter from behind the fallen poles. A dense unpleasant smell arose from beneath the ruins about two standing walls and drifted out across the narrow road on the chilly wind. *"Tod,"* said the mother under her breath. Side by side they stared down the uneven grey slopes to where the brick-red remains of the institution sprawled in the glittering light.

"What's that?" asked Selvaggia.

"That's where they used to keep the crazy people." The pointed head nodded.

Many, many years before, a woman doctor had spoken to Balamir in those same buildings:

"What's your name?"

"Will you tell me what day this is?"

"Weiss nicht."

"Do you know what year this is?"

"Do you know where you are?"

"Weiss nicht."

"You're going to have a good time here."

"Weiss nicht, weiss nicht!"

As they went down the hill the bright sun had become more cold, their feet were wet, and they had been very glad to get back to the quiet of the rooms.

The yellow walls flickered as the electric globe dimmed, rose, dimmed but did not go out, as the generator sputtered and continued to drone far beneath us in Balamir's basement. Below her stomach the white flesh puffed into a gentle mound, then dissolved into the sheets, while her fingers against my arm traced over the silken outlines of a previous wound. Her mind could only see as far as immediate worry for her son, never awoke in anticipation for the after-dark, or in fear to rise in light; and as the thought of the child slipped downwards and ceased, every moment hence was plotted by actions circled about in the room. She tapped my arm as if to say, "I get up, but don't bother," and left the couch, the top of the robe swinging behind from the waist. She poured the cold water into the basin, washed carefully and left the water to settle. In the other room to get a light for my cigarette, she said, *"Schlaf',"* to her daughter at the window and returned with the lighted splinter. In his sleep the Census-Taker heard a few low mournful notes of a horn, as if an echo, in a deeper register, of the bugles that used to blast fitfully out among the stunted trees in the low fields on the south edge of town. Once, twice, then Herr Stintz stood his instrument in a corner and sat alone in the dark on the floor below. The apartment on the second floor was dark.

"They're dancing tonight," I said, paper stuck to my lips, "let's go, I still have a few hours."

"Tanzen?"

"Yes. Let's go, just for a while."

She dressed in a pale blue gown that sparkled in the wrinkles, stepped into the shoes of yesterday's walk and washed again. I wore no tie but buttoned the grey shirt up to my throat, rubbed my eyes, and reaching over, shook the Census-Taker by the foot. The hallway was completely black and ran with cold drafts. We went slowly from the fifth to the fourth, to the third, the second, the Census-Taker leaning with both arms on the rail.

"The Duke's," said Jutta, nodding.

"Ah, the Duke's."

The little girl heard the door slam shrilly far below her vigil at the window.

"What's all this about dancing?" asked the Census-Taker, his hands held tightly over his ears from the cold, his raised elbows jerking in peculiar half-arcs with his stride. We walked quickly to the hill that rose much higher in the darkness.

At night the institution towered upward crookedly, and fanned out into a haphazard series of dropped terraces and barren rooms, suddenly twisted walls and sealed entrances, combed of reality, smothered out of all order by its overbearing size. We walked at an average pace, feeling for each other's hands, unafraid of this lost architecture, unimpressed by the sound of our own feet. There was no food in the vaulted kitchens. Offices and conference rooms were stripped of pencils, records, leather cushions. Large patches of white wall were smeared with dilating lost designs of seeping water, and inner doors were smeared with chalk fragments of situation reports of the then anxious and struggling Allied armies. The institution was menacing, piled backwards on itself in chaotic slumber, and in segregated rooms, large tubs—long, fat and thick edges ringed with metal hooks that once held patients on their canvas cradles —had become sooted with grey, filled with fallen segments of plaster from the ceilings. Strange, unpursued animals now made their lairs in the corners of the dormitories where insulin had once flowed and produced cures. And this was where the riot had taken place.

Each of us walking through this liberated and lonely sanctum, past its now quiet rooms, heard fragments of recognition in the bare trees. For once it had been both awesome and yet holy, having caused in each of us, silent marchers, at one time or another, a doubt for his own welfare and also a momentary wonder at the way they could handle all those patients. Once the days had been interrupted by the very hours and the place had passed by our minds new and impressive with every stroke. But now the days were uninterrupted and the shadows from the great felled wings sprawled colorless and without any voice about our ever moving feet. Then, scudding away through the maze, new, unkempt and artificial, the low clapboard storehouse emerged, champing of strange voices. It heeled, squat beneath its own glimmers of weak light, a small boarded place of congregation, hounded by the darkness of the surrounding buildings.

Without slacking pace, we neared the din and fray above the scratching needle, the noise of women dancing with women, and men with men, shadows skipping without expression across the blind of a half-opened door. They ceased to whirl only for a moment and then the feet shuffled again over the floor boards, and we, walking towards the building, smelled the odor of damp cinders and felt for a moment the black leaves settle about our ankles.

Jutta, the Census-Taker and myself, emerging from flat darkness into light that was only a shade brighter, bowed our heads, fending off the tinted glare that filled the spaces between the rigid dancers. Close together, we stood for a moment sunken in the doorway. Figures stepped forwards, backwards, caught in a clockwork of custom, a way of moving that was almost forgotten. Gathered in the storehouse, back to back, face measured to face, recalled into the group and claiming name instead of number, each figure, made responsible, appeared with the same sackcloth idleness as Jutta. They swung out of the mist and appeared with pocketed cheeks and shaven heads. They seemed to dance with one leg always suspended, small white bodies colliding like round seamless pods, and fingers entwined were twice as long as palms. They danced continuously forming patterns, always the same, of grey and pale blue. The beauties were already sick, and the word *krank* passed from group to group over devious tongues, like the grapevine current of fervent criminal words that slide through wasted penal colonies. The smallest women had the roundest legs that bounced against jutting knees, and the seams of their gowns were taken up with coarse thread. High above their shoulders towered their partners' heads, loose, with cold whitening eyes, tongues the faded color of cheeks, curled back to the roots of forgotten words. Several girls were recently orphaned when Allied trucks, bringing German families back from hiding, had smashed, traveling too fast along the highway, and had scattered the old people like punched cows in the fields. Some of these danced together, stopping to see which way the other would turn.

I touched Jutta's hand and we walked into the center of the floor while, leaning against the wall, the Census-Taker watched, trying to recall each passing couple. Jutta leaned and pushed, hung to my hand, stepped now upon my own foot, now upon another's, and the stiff waltz whispered out of the machine. The Czechs, Poles and Belgians danced just as she, their wooden shoes sticking to the floor, wearing the same blue dresses with faded dots, some with bones broken off-center, some with armpits ringed as black as soot. For it was not the Germans who thought of coming together when there was nothing to say, when no one could understand the vast honored ideal swept under; it was the rest of Europe—bedridden with idleness, dumb with tremendous distance, unhealthy in confinement, these gathered in the storehouse—who had begun this dance in the evenings. A few true Germans were scattered among them. Men wandered through, seeking a girl they had lost. These men, startled and old, still wore unironed hospital gowns as shirts, moved ready to push the others aside with delicate arms, walked with their feet in sandals and with smoke-white faces. A young girl, sitting on a bench, gently rubbed her hands over an Italian officer's trousers while he leaned back, his eyes closed, and she, smiling, watched the circle of dancers and smelled the boneless herring on his breath.

There was no drink to be had in the storehouse. The smell of pasteboard and dust hovered over the walls, Russian ex-soldiers grinned at each other like Mongolians in a corner, a half-French girl with tangled colorless hair, pregnant with a paunch beneath her belt, looked ugly and out of place; all were spiritless from the very strangeness of the country and so they crowded themselves, unwanted, into this end of town. All of them slept in the back rooms on hay that should have been fed to the herds.

In the brick building nearest the storehouse, Balamir had lain half-awake, sometimes in the mornings, or in the late afternoons when flowers were closing, in one of the large tubs, all but his head submerged in water the temperature of blood, and behind him had heard the waiting nurse who flipped the pages of a magazine. The evenings sidled through the long green shade, towels hung like mats from the walls. He was surprised to find that his hands floated. And always the pages flipping one on the other, pages beating just behind his head. The water gurgled out of the tub, disturbing the peace and quiet, the shaded air of the small room.

Through the minutes, the dancers were the same long lines of inmates stamping time to the phonograph, dancing in block-like groups with arms that were too long. In the back rooms, a few figures sprawled on the bunks overcome with an inexcusable exhaustion, weak and helpless under the low makeshift roof of the storehouse. Overhead the stars were clear.

"Shall we rest?"

"I only have a while more. Let's dance." She followed me. Jutta did not know that she looked like the others, that here in public no one knew the dress was washed, that her face, ribboned with long hair, was just as unkempt and unpleasant as the other tottering faces. If I had left her for a moment and then returned, she would not have known who her partner was, but looking over shoulders that were all alike, she would have danced on.

"Is it going to be difficult?"

"No."

I, Zizendorf, like all men, was similar to her husband who had been captured, but it was something indefinable that made me particularly similar. The other men's sleeves were too short, their heads too thin and bare, all actually unlike her husband; yet they were similar in a way, because seeing them she had started on the long glorious path, then had forgotten a great deal. But I was different from them all and was better for her than her husband.

She gussed that the hall might become empty soon and she would be alone. The shoulder was hard under the cloth, her back began to feel stiff and it was difficult not to go to sleep. A figure in a tight green suit kept changing the record, wiping it with a piece of rag. And in one of the back rooms smelling of flour that had long since been hauled away, where some sprawled or sat by windows streaked with dirt, a girl crouched on all fours, her head hanging forward, face covered with hair, the back of her neck shining like a small round coin, and clutched the sides of the bunk in motionless indecision. Down the corridor we danced, trooped like men about to change the guard, voices low and serious. White heads in pairs that were the same size, shape, identical bony structures, came together in the damp place and kissed. The girl lost her hold, fell forward and, face buried in a wrinkled grey shirt, tried to sleep.

Under my arm I felt the pistol, in my head faintly heard the shrill music, and dancing with Jutta, I felt as well as I ever felt. Naturally my eyes looked from face to face, beyond the back of her head, followed the girls that were hugged along and passed from dry smile to smile. It stirred a memory of burnished Paris women and silver bars during the second part of my visit, of murky waters stirred with blinking lights and faint odors of flowers on street corners. I bumped a man and no words were spoken, then I was pushed backwards into a girl and tried to recall the sensation—while all about me moved the bundles of rags, grass sticking to their collars.

The Census-Taker had lost us and squeezed on the end of a narrow bench that sagged with girls whose fingers were chewed at the ends. He looked with distaste from one red knee to another. He hooked his fingers in his shirt and tried to rest his back, felt something soft and loose pushing into his side and pushed away. An Italian with long hair down his neck looked from the Census-Taker to the girl, and catching his eye, shook an olive head "no," in a meaningful way; the Census-Taker shut his eyes.

The lilt and strain moved back and forth in an endless way, foreshadowed and stunted in careless glances, in the unexcited hang of a dress, with words partially exposed to hearing, with all their mixed nationality running out in shuffling footsteps. Something inside me motioned to hold her closer, and I did so, the scratching close now to my ear. I lit a cigarette with one arm hooked around her neck, the flame close to her hair, spaces black between my teeth as I exhaled. Two of the white heads hung together in a corner with breaths stifled, while the music rested on the constant low scuffle of wooden shoes.

"I must leave," I said. My hand rested on the middle of her back; I looked at her kindly. Something about my person could still be called *soldat* but not the crawling, unshaven *soldatto* filth of the Italians who wriggled dog-fashion.

"Yes," she answered. In the Census-Taker's dis- . turbed sleep, the white handkerchief, recently blown into, fluttered down like a child's parachute to the ground.

"You must get him back to the rooms. Be careful not to fall. Get some sleep, you look tired. I'll come and see you in the morning after it's done, and remember, there's no danger." She smelled a breath of tobacco as my cheek touched her forehead for a moment, and I stepped off, no longer recognized, among the grey masqueraders. Alone, Jutta followed the length of three walls, past outstretched thick feet, past bodies hanging arm in arm, until she found where the Census-Taker was sitting, the last in a row of tallow girls. Gently, holding beneath one arm, she made him rise until his strong breath fumed about her throat, until his red eyes were narrowed full on her face, and speaking softly, she propelled him along. Feeling the narrow doorway, they found themselves out in the night air, alone. In the receding storehouse, the dancers massed together in the cold tart atmosphere to perform, couple by couple all night, some distasteful ritual, whereby those with uncovered bellies and tousled hair walked in their midst as easily and unnoticed as the most infected and sparkling damsel.

Jutta's son, the fairy, fled for his life, his knees the size of finger-joints whirling in every direction like the un-coordinated thrashings of a young and frightened fox.

The Duke continued to prod and tap with the gleaming cane, drew the coat tighter about his chest.

Jutta's daughter watched in the window, her golden curls tight like a wig about the narrow face.

Jutta herself, with the Census-Taker heavily against her shoulders, started down the cinder path, while over all the town and sty-covered outskirts hung a somber, early, Pentecostal chill. She moved slowly because the man mumbled thickly in her ear and his feet caught against the half-buried bricks that lined the path. Finally she could no longer hear the music and was quickly back in the thick deserted kingdom of crumbling buildings and roosting birds, the asylum all about her. She wanted to get home to sleep.

I followed, far ahead of them, the clay contours of the railroad tracks, crossed the wooden scaffold over the canal, smelled the rivulets of fog, heard the slapping of deflated, flat rubber boats against the rocks, made my way across ruts and pieces of shattered wood. I knew that soon the American on the motorcycle, the only Allied overseer in this part of Germany, would be passing through the town, shivering with cold, mud-covered and trembling, hunched forward over the handle bars, straining with difficulty to see the chopped-up road in the darkness. The main highway, cracked badly from armored convoys, crossed the town at a sharp bend where the low wet fields faced the abrupt end of a few parallel streets of shapeless brick houses. A log lay across the road, heavy and invisible. For a moment, I remembered my true love, and then I was following the rough line of the log, leaving the town behind, and slipping in haste, I dropped down beside the two soft murmuring voices and leaned against the steep embankment.

"He'll be here soon."

"Ja, der Tod."

Backs to the road, we looked out across the endless grey fields and almost expected to see barrels of smoke and the red glare of shooting flares through the twisted stunted trees.

Jutta could not believe that I was in danger, but some dull warning voice seemed to try to speak from the leaning buildings, and the Census-Taker babbled in her ear; some voice, a consideration, tried to force its way through her blunted journey. As she passed the building where Balamir had once been kept, she felt this new twist in things and did not want to lose me. Years before she would have seen the face pressed to the window and would have heard from his lips what was in her heart: "I don't want to see those birds smashed!" Balamir first screamed so long ago to his startled nurse. Jutta hurried, pushing the drunk man in front of her towards the hill, and began to think that Stella was a strange woman to take a man crazy with the stars into the house, while out in the cold, I, her lover, had to wait for the puttering of the motor-bike, for the saddlebags, the prize.

PART TWO—1914

LOVE

"Stella sings like an angel," cried the crowd, and the
Bavarian orchestra played all the louder. Some of
them were shocked, some annoyed, others opened
their big hearts and wanted to join in the chorus,
while some looked out into the sultry night. The
largest of them were eager waiters whose black
jackets showed here and there with darker patches
of velvet from stains, whose stout arms bore platters
of beer and who paused near the kitchen doors to
hear the new singer. The officers in their new grey
tunics were slightly smaller and the girls were smaller
yet—but still were Nordic women, straight, blonde,
strong and unsupple. Even the vines on the trellises
were thick and round, swaying only slightly out in
the heat. Heads nodded close together at the tables
in the garden. In the brightly-lit room the wooden
chairs and tables were uncarved, unornamented, and
the white walls and pillared ceiling were remote. It
did not seem possible that enough blue smoke and
shadow could rise to make the hall alluring. The men
talked together, the clatter of cups intruded. Their
backs were straight, they nodded cordially, and the
light gleamed on undecorated chests. But it was only
ten, still dusk, still formal. They smiled. Stella
twisted the handkerchief in her fingers, squeezed it
strongly into her damp palms and continued to sing
and to smile. Then she found it simple, found that
her throat opened and her head could turn and

smile, that she could move about and thrust into her shoulders the charm of the song. They listened, turned away, then listened again, and like a girl with breeding and a girl with grace, she made them look and sang to them. First, sadly, then with her eyes bright and her shoulders thrust backwards:

"Dass du mich liebst, weiss ich."

Some of them laughed and twisted in their seats. She shook her hair loose, she felt like telling them they could come to her, that they could send flowers.

"Must I then, must I then come back to your heart
  And smile again?"

She moved as if she had a sunflower just beneath her bosom, as if she could draw them sailing on a sacred lake, and first a crackling chicken, then a duckling, then a head of cheese fell under her swoop. But always she looked directly over into their eyes startled from eating, or eyes large from some private imagination. Her bosom, larger than her hips, swayed with pleasure. And only a moment before she had stood in the left wing, hidden by dusty curtains and sheets of music, feeling that never in the world could she face the lights and attention of the drinking hall. The *Sportswelt Brauhaus,* austere and licensed, patronized and rushed upon, coldly kept her out for a moment, then with a smart burst from the accordion, drew her down, deeply as possible, into the fold. After the summer broke, she had come, and tonight she stood before them all, her body slowly showing through the gown, more and more admired for her stately head, singing,

"All my body blossoms with a greater . . ."

They clapped, chuckled, and slowly the undecorated chests slid open, the lights swirled about in the fog, while Stella, arm around the accordion player, sang anything at all that came to mind. Her ancestors had run berserk, cloaked themselves in animal skins, carved valorous battles on their shields, and several old men, related thinly in blood from a distant past, had jumped from a rock in Norway to their death in the sea. Stella, with such a history running thickly in her veins, caught her breath and flung herself at the feet of her horned and helmeted kinsmen, while the Bavarians schnitzled back and forth in a drunken trio.

In an alley behind the hall timbered with consecrated ash, the darkness and odor of wet stone rose in spirals of steam as from below a horse on a winter's day. The sound of the violin, jumping dangerously along the length of the alley walls, merged with the basso wheezing of a lascivious merchant and swept overhead into the heat of the garden.

Ernie, the *Brauhaus* owner's son, shuffled his feet to two dry spots, leaned his shoulder against the slippery rock, and steadied his face covered with dueling scars, down into the green darkness. Stella's unknown, unnamed voice, beginning to reach the crown of her triumph, leaped straight from the small bright window behind his back and fell about the heads of those in the garden, dumb with love. Ernie wiped his hands on his trousers, leaned back and looked up into the sweltering night, his pockets stuffed with hundred mark notes, his eyes blind to the flickering sky. He saw only emptiness in the

43

day's returns, felt the scratches from a skillful bout burn on his cheek. His tongue was thick and numb with beer. The Merchant, barely afloat in the humid atmosphere, still cradling jade and ivory blocks in his arms and girded with a Turkish robe, made a perfect soft target in the darkness. Ernie breathed in and out on the same air, the pig's tail lay heavily on his stomach, and he gave no thought to steel blades or the Merchant's fat bulk. Howls of laughter were muffled inside the hall, low voices floated over the garden wall in tones that said there was something to hide, and the heady smell of tulips, roses, German-valor-petals, hydrangeas and cannon flowers sank into the pea-green pit of stench at his feet. The flowers turned their pistils out to catch the rain if it should come, the Merchant's breath drew closer, and the moon shone once in the heavens, loaded like a sac with water.

Ernie squeezed his left hand, the hand with the last two fingers gone from a hatchet stroke, into his pocket tight with bills, and turned back towards the light, towards the free men of the hall. He would sit on a worshipped pile of granite, a small duelist in the hall of kings. The Merchant tried to follow but, like a laboring hind, slipped and fell, his fat body dragging along over the stones. He could not call out and each time he moved he slid deeper. Ernie heard his thudding fall and walked faster, trying to find again a place for light and song. He measured his steps and seemed to tread upon the whole world of Germany as he walked, half-consciously, back near the aurora of tabled clans, disciplined faces, and all the irony and fellowship of his men-at-arms. A man in grey staggered past, ready with malice or with a bow at the waist, and far in the back of the alley Ernie heard him trip against the fallen Merchant, heard a muffled word against the background of summer nightbirds.

Ernie, because of the fingers gone from his hand and the ugly sight of three remaining claws, could never ride a black mare into the din of volleying balls, or crawl hand over hand through the wet fields of Belgium. He touched the middle and forefinger with the thumb and heard the woman's voice crying out to the men young in soul. Inside he sat at his father's table under the shadows and far to the rear, and melting into the crowd became nondescript, feigned to strike out with ignored curt expressions.

Stella, like her father, held them at bay; and, losing one by one those traits that were hers, absorbed more and more the tradition that belonged to all. She did not lisp when she sang, but boomed the words in an unnatural voice. And the gestures she developed came with ease. She walked from the archway of her father's house to the audience of the *Sportswelt* transgressing natural thought as clearly as she passed the stages of the months. She, the sorceress, sent them boiling and held them up for joy, feeling pain only in the last moment before sleep, half-dressed, on the bedroom floor. Gerta, the nurse, thought the Devil had come a long way from the forest to find her. Every dress she owned, every male plate of armor, every bone comb and silken ban, was stamped with the seal of the camp follower, and screaming in nightmares to the dead ears of her sleeping father, she followed the weeks of 1914. Beneath her eyes she had painted indigo stains as if she had been beaten, and her eyes swept from tall black trees to the glaciers of dead warriors, green with the tint of pine trees, sober with a longing that came of eighteen years of summer patios and a partition of a princely nursery.

After the last chorus of the song, she bowed straight-legged from her flaring hips, flushed to their applause, and made her way to old Herr Snow's table, storing appreciation up in her heart, storing each face beside the photograph of the white flaking head of Gerta, the nurse. Blue smoke floated above the sawdust and the tide of conversation rolled in the lion cage. She sat where Herr Snow, with his red beard, indicated, felt his wrists slide her smoothly forward until she touched the table. She looked from face to face. "You were excellent," he said. "This is my son, Ernst, who enjoys your singing so much." Ernie, thin and more alive with beer, pushed back his chair and nodded, fixed her as he might have fixed a rosy-cheeked sister, adult and come alive from his free past. "And," said Herr Snow, "this is Mr. Cromwell, a guest of mine." Mr. Cromwell smiled with an easy drunken grace and filled her glass. He did not miss the charm of London or of the English countryside rollicking in summer but slept late and heard no cocks crowing in the early dawn.

"You're English?" asked Stella.

"Yes, but I particularly like Germany. The lakes and cities seem like vistas cut into the ice age. You sing well."

Herr Snow was proud of Ernie because his other son, a boy of nine, forever wore his head strapped in a brace, and the words that came from the immovable mouth came also from a remote frightening world. Old Snow, prosperous and long owner of the *Sportswelt*, looked with hard admiration on Ernie's face, saw his own eyes and nose staring resentfully back. With mute excitement, Stella followed each jagged crevice of the scars, noticed how they dug beneath the cheeks highlighting the bones, how the eyes were pressed between encroaching blocks of web-like tissue. She waited for the three claws of the left hand to close talon-like just above her knee, grew warm to the close-kept face down in its corner. The orchestra filled out the room behind her, roasted apples fell from the bosom of an oracle, burnt and golden, and gradually the three men drew closer, warm with all the taste of a chivalric age. She covered the glass before her with the golden hair and saw for a moment in its swirling depths, the naked cowardice of the fencer, the future fluttering wings of the solitary British plane leaving its token pellet in the market place, her mother's body rolling around it like a stone stained forever, the stain becoming dry and black as onyx.

The rain had begun to fall and the summer thunder drifted over the wet leaves, coursed over the darkened glistening steeples. The carriage rocked to and fro, water splashing from the wheels, dripping from the deep enclosures of passing doors. They traveled slowly down *die Heldenstrasse,* hearing only the soft rain, the chopping of the steel hoofs, the smooth movements of leather. Oiled gunmetal springs swung them easily through the June night while Mephistopheles, crouching in a choir-room, circled this eighteenth day of the month in red. He, in his black cowl, called the sleeping swans to pass by them on the lake in the park and the coachman flicked the whip over the horse's ears.

"Why did you want to take me home?" she asked.

"I'm fond of the color of your hair and eyes."

Stella felt nothing near her, could feel no man or

beast or spirit lurking under the rain, no hand crept towards hers. She could not even feel or hear his breathing, only the steady turning of the axletree. No man in the world, sitting as Cromwell sat, soft felt brim curling with rain, fine straight features and wide nostrils drinking in the lavender, no such man or leader of men could have caused a single ripple in her even tone.

"Why didn't you stay home, in your English home?" Her hair was becoming damp and heavy.

"Home? Why I don't really have a home, and in fact, I don't believe anyone has." Now, with a change of wind, she could smell his scented breath, but he was foreign, unreal, was a humor she could brush away with her white hand. "I feel that I am one of those middle-aged men whom, in a little while, people will call an expatriate." In full light he looked a little old, resembled a smart but tottering wolfhound guarding its own grave. And Cromwell, like a change of mind or a false impression, like an unexpected meeting or a mistake in the dark, filled Ernie's place and caused in Stella a fleeting disbelief; she expected to see the lacerated face aloof in the corner of her carriage. He rode as an Archduke, unconsciously wiping the rain from his waistcoat, smiling slightly with lonely intoxication. Stella looked beyond the figure of the fat coachman to see the angular street unwind.

"I think that everyone has a home." Her voice was musical like the axletree.

When he spoke, it was not quite as if he wanted to talk to her. His throat was hidden by an upturned flowing collar.

"I, for one, don't even remember my mother's face. England is a land of homeless people, but the

Germans, though just as homeless, are a little slow in realizing it. And besides, they have a beautiful capacity for ideals of conquest, a traditional hero-ism." His mouth was becoming heavy with a very sour taste of sleep, a taste of finding it still dark beyond the raised shade, the sourness accumulated from many unwanted meals, and still he kept his head in a smiling manner, looked into the flowering darkness with a pleasant friendly way of practiced youth.

"The bedclothes, curtains, my mother's gowns, the very way I looked as a child, were always unfamiliar. Unfamiliar."

The slight layer of accent beneath his perfect speech began to disrupt her isolation. The soft ribbon of street started to break up into glaring bricks, into actual corners, into black patches of shadow against the curb, the horse stumbling and nodding. The rain shook in the linden trees.

"You should have stayed home," she said. Stella thought that she was too precious for this journey and counted, one by one, the statues of Heroes that lined the street on the park side and wished she could recognize the stone faces. They seemed like metal behind an angry crowd, as if they might step out to march up the stifling street, rain falling from their foreheads. Almost like man and wife they plodded along in silence, the late night growing smoky, their clothes wet as if they had been playfully wading in the park lake. How wonderful that they had all liked her singing, that they had clapped and looked after her, that she could sing to State heroes. Somehow she thought that Cromwell had not clapped at all. Again she could almost feel the three claws just above her knee, would offer her firm leg

49

to their frightened touch. Cromwell, though he seemed to be easily considering the black early morning, found that he could not settle back, resigned to the rain, easily riding in the Duchess' carriage, but felt a vague general pain as if the Heroes followed him. He wondered what the Krupp gun would do to Europe, saw the Swiss sliding down the mountains on their seats, saw the English bobbing in the Channel, and saw the rest of the nations falling in line like a world-wide pestilence.

She had seen Ernst for the first time a few mornings ago, out in the empty garden behind the *Sportswelt,* watching the blue shadows give place to the bright rising sun, neither English, Swiss nor German, but a fighter without his trappings, dangling his legs from an upturned chair. She knew he was a coward when the old man screamed out of the window, "Ernst, Ernst," in a loud bellowing unhappy voice that did not have to command respect. But he jumped, stared at the quiet blank wall of the building, and then she knew that it might have been she herself who called, and she laughed behind the shadow of the open window when it bellowed again, "Ernst, Ernst, *kommst du hier.*" She could tell by the way his head moved that his eyes must be frightened, that all his frail arms and legs would be trembling. He was magnificent! She watched him throw the foil from him and it rolled into a flower bed, lay beneath the drooping petals. But she knew that his face was tough, she could see that the blood would be rising into his head, that his ugly hand would be twitching. The garden became Valhalla, he could kill somebody with a single quick movement, and she wanted to be with him in Valhalla. She heard the door slam and the old man's voice rolling angrily out. The flowers turned very bright in the sun; she could, at that moment, sing her heart out. When she saw Herr Snow a while later he was perfectly calm.

The musty odor of the wet carriage mixed with the lavender of Cromwell's hair, the Heroes passed out of view.

"I don't think you should have come with me," she said into the coachman's back.

"You must give me a chance," Cromwell answered, thinking of the vast Rhineland, "after all, I'm homeless."

On a few isolated occasions in his life, Ernie had been swept into overwhelming crisis, and, after each moment of paralysis, had emerged more under his father's thumb than ever. He remembered that his mother, with her tight white curls and slow monotonous movement, had never succumbed, but had always yielded, to the deep irritable voice. Her kind but silent bulk had slowly trickled down his father's throat, easing the outbursts of his violent words, until at last, on a hot evening, they had laid her away in the back yard, while his young brother, head already in the brace, had crawled along at their sides, screaming and clutching at his trousers. His father loved him with the passionate control of a small monarch gathering and preening his five-man army, and only used him as a scapegoat to vent an angry desire for perfection. The old man would have wept in his hands if anything had happened to Ernie, and, as ruler of the *Sportswelt* and surrounding Europe, had given him every opportunity for love. Ernie, dwarfed at his side, sat every evening at the back table in the hall, until, when the stately patrons rolled with laughter and the father became more absorbed in them than in his son, he could slip away and match swords with those as desperate as himself. "You'll get yourself killed," his father would say, "they're cutting you apart bit by bit."

His father had forced one of the few small crises himself the only time he saw his son in combat. They were fencing in a grove several miles from the city, the sun raising steam about their feet, fencing with a violent hatred and determination. They were alone, stripped to the waist, scratches and nicks bleeding on their chests, heads whirling with the heat. The Baron, young, agile, confident, drove him in and out of the trees to stick him a thousand times before actually wounding him. Ernie was sick, fought back, but saw blades through the fogged goggles. Herr Snow came upon the scene like a fat indignant judge, his face white with rage. He wrenched the weapon from the Baron's hand and beating him without mercy across the shoulders and buttocks, drove him screaming from the grove, tiring his thick arm with the work. "You're a god damn fool," he told his son.

Ernie walked in a dark trimmer's night for a long while and in the *Sportswelt* heard the bees buzzing with a low vicious hum. Since he was a Shylock, his face grew tight and bitter and Herr Snow took to keeping a lighted candle by his bed. Even asleep, Ernie's feet jiggled up and down as they had danced in the grove, the bulk of the noble crushing swiftly down on him, and in a frenzy Ernie jabbed quicker and quicker at the raging white face of his father, fell back weeping beneath the heavy broadsword.

"Well," and the words pushed themselves over the end of a wet sausage, "why didn't you take her home yourself? You'll not get any women just sitting with me." Ernie made a move to leave.

"Wait. Just let me tell you that once your mother

looked at me, there was no other man." He held the stein like a scepter. "You want to go for these," his hands made awkward expressive movements around his barrel chest. Herman Snow had not only used his hands but had made tender love to the silent woman and asked dearly for her hand on his knees that were more slender in those days. He thought her sad face more radiant than the sun, and worshipped her as only a German could. On the evenings when she had a headache he stroked her heavy hair and said, *"Ja, Liebling, ja, Liebling,"* over and over a hundred times in his softest voice. They had taken a trip on a canal barge owned by his brother. Herman had propped her in the stern on coarse pillows, away from the oil-smeared deck forward and the guttural voices of the crew, and she had looked warmly with interest on the passing flat country as if they were sailing on the Nile. Herman gazed into her face, held one of the strong hands.

"A little aggression is needed," said the old man. Ernie lost his head in the stein and remembered the fat Merchant, like Herman, like papa, sprawled out in the alley with a string of women behind him and children gorging themselves on attention, sprawled like a murdered Archduke, his face in the bile. The hall was finally game, the troops screamed and stamped feet, dolls with skirts drawn above pink garters perched on elephant knees suggesting the roar of mighty Hannibal. Old Herman made fast excursions into the crowd, urging, interested. "Hold her tighter, more beer, more beer," and returned to the stoop-shouldered Ernie with his face alive in enjoyment. Several times Ernie thought he could hear Stella's voice above the howling, and like an assassin under floodlights, he shivered.

53

"Don't be such a fearful *Kind,*" said Herman, puffing with excitement, "join the chase." He smiled momentarily at his son above the strenuous noise of the orchestra. When he left the table again to encourage a maenadic blonde and an old general, Ernie rushed from the prosperous Valhalla.

Rain filled his eyes with warm blurred vision, filled his outward body with the heat of his mind, and running until his breathing filled his ears, he clattered past opulent swaying wet branches, past windows opening on endless sleep. "Ernst, Ernst," the summer evening cried and he dashed zig-zag up the broad boulevard, raced to outrun the screaming, raced to catch the dog who rode with her away, raced to coincide with Princip in Sarajevo. He ran to spend energy, tried to run his own smallness into something large, while far in the distance he thought he heard the carriage wheels. If he could spread before her the metal of magnificence, if he could strike lightning from the sky, if he could only arrest her for one brief moment in the devotion he felt whirling in the night. But then the past told him the Merchant, or the Baron, or Herman would steal her off to a nest of feathers—before he could speak.

He felt that his belt would burst, and so, just before reaching the line of Heroes, he stopped in the park. He thought that his mother would see, would stand looking at him in the dark, so he pushed behind the foliage, behind a bush that scratched at his fumbling hands. The rain became stronger and stronger and still he was rooted behind the bush, desperation on his face to be off, to be flying. Then he was running through the shadows like a flapping bird. When he passed the line of statues, each Hero gave him a word to harden his heart: *love, Stella,*

Ernst, lust, tonight, leader, land. He felt that if old Herman ran at his side, he would tell him to get her in the britches. Already the guns were being oiled and the Belgians, not he, would use that Merchant as a target.

"Tomorrow you'll wake up and find we're in a war," said Cromwell. The carriage was turning the last corner, he turned his ready benevolence on the cruel castles, thought he'd like to tell his old father, but that was impossible.

"Then you'll go home?" she asked.

"No. I think I'll stay. It is pleasant, in moments such as these, knowing with certainty an approaching catastrophe, to view the whole incident that will probably extend fifty years, not as the death of politics or the fall of kings and wives, but as the loyalty of civilization, to realize that Krupp, perhaps a barbarian, is more the peg where history hangs than a father who once spoke of honor. If I could get into my father's house, past his fattening memory, I would tell him what's coming and leave him something to carry away with him."

"I, on the other hand, star of maidenhood, having found love, want to tell my father nothing, and if your prophecy should fall on our heads, could do nothing but protect my own. If in this hour of crisis, we must ride side by side, I will become, as you wish, your Archduchess for the people, but where your eyes and theirs cannot look, I am arrogant."

They were none the closer when they heard his running footsteps, when they looked in fear, back to the road they had just traveled, looked quickly over the low rear of the carriage. He ran up to them gasping out of the darkness, clutched the side of the carriage as if to hold it in his hand, and at that moment a bevy of disturbed birds chirped vividly in fright. They did not recognize him, did not speak, and for a moment, Cromwell waited to see the short muzzle of the pistol, to feel his ears enveloped in concussion, and on impulse almost took her in his arms for the last time. But the carriage continued, the coachman sleeping, and the assailant was dragged, half-running, half-stumbling, veins exploding around his eyes. Then, in great deliberation, she leaned and touched his fingers.

"Come, get in," she said.

"No, no, I cannot."

Cromwell was a fool. He wouldn't move, but back straight, hat over his eyes, he sat and waited. His gloved hands trembled on his knees. "I'll come back," Ernst said and once more took to his heels as the carriage reached the curb and a crowd seemed to gather. Stella knew, in this dark disrupted haze, that she was somewhere near her greatest love. Francis Ferdinand lay on the seat of the carriage, his light shirt filled with blood, his epaulettes askew and on the floor lay the body of his departed wife, while the assassin, Gavrilo Princip, ran mad through the encircling streets. Obviously the advent of the great war would not throw them all together, make them friends, or even make them enemies; Ernie was ready, even in the throes of love, for a goal of religious fanaticism; Cromwell simply longed, desperately, to fit into the conflict somewhere; and Stella knew only that she was climbing high and would someday lose him. It all started as simply as the appearance of Ernie's dangerous, unpleasant face. When the people found out, the people of Bosnia, Austria, and the Hapsburg monarchy, they caused a silent, spreading, impersonal commotion over the body of Ferdinand.

"Thank you," said Stella.

"Oh, I'll be around." She did not turn to watch Cromwell go back to the carriage.

The University was black, impressive, most of its archives and bare rooms encased in a drawn restless wine-stupor, part of its jagged face grey, menacing, piled backwards on itself in chaotic slumber. The rain came down in broken sheets covering first one roof, then a ledge, then splashing against a swinging door, sluicing down the crumbling channels, smothering dust-filled caves crawling with larvae. The center of revolution, dogma and defeat, it drew the city into its walls with a crushing will; and behind its ancient and topheavy porticos and crags, behind small windows and breathing flues, lodged the uninhibited, the young, the old. Ernie crossed a hollow court, dodged down ecclesiastical alleys past flowing fonts, made his way past stone connecting arches and hybrid walls, hastened beyond a mausoleum of brain to where the stone eruption gave way to a wooden comb of corridors. Resolved to upset his dying fall, he finally lunged at a solid door, smelled the dank unvarying stench of huddled students and counted forward five doors while the summer rain rolled thickly down the stained windows, and his footfalls still called back from the stone. The door was covered with the prints of ancient nervous fingers, was damp with the palms that had slipped in and out for centuries. Heavy furniture and eaten rug, iron candle holders and unused loving chair, were pushed into dust-covered heaps lining three walls, leaving the scarred floor a wide cold arena, colorless beneath the only lamp that burned in the University, peopled by the only waking men. They slouched, sleepless, like a band of raiders in a thick wood, drinking a colorless water that caused the lungs to heave, the skin to burn, that brought violent images before the eyes. The single light threw stiff unyielding shadows on the horse-collared masks, on the molding chest mats, protective of bowels, front and loins, covered with dry rust and rattling buckles, grey wire-like stuffing from rough slashes.

The Baron, older in time, more vicious and less proud with his bastard Spanish-German head thrust back and upwards at the agony-carved rafters, more hot and princely and dog-like under his eyes and stripped arms, waited until precisely the proper moment when the eyes found their two-sided common target, when the arena drifted with unraked ashes, to slip to his knees and draw as in sleep a weapon from the debris. The onlookers let the liquor trickle down their nostrils, coughed, rubbed their collars, stared with their mouths open in hate. These were the agates that could not grow.

In the first moment their bodies lost form, clashing like roosters with spiked heels, aiming at brief exposed patches of white, striking for scarecrow targets. They struck at the *Physik* of limbs. In the second moment, the arena stained with drops of ink, walls resounding with blows, they aimed at the perilous eyes and ears, the delicate tendons of the neck, fingers, stabbing at the *Kultur* of sense, and a blade-tip sang past his lower lip, splitting the skin the length of his under jaw. In the third moment they found the groin, and he felt a pain from the acci-

dental flat of the blade that traveled from the ab-
domen to his throat in a brief spasm, the original
Unlust. He stooped, and the bell of the saber rang
through the ashes, dropped to the floor in a finished
scoop. Then gradually he began to fall from a high,
blunted indefinable space where the Hero's words:
love, Stella, Ernst, lust, tonight, leader, land revolved
out of relation, until he finally reached particulars too
extreme to comprehend. Brine filled the hollow of
his gum, the cuticle of one thumb bled into a purple
half-moon, and an internal kink filled him with pain
from the stomach to the blind gut. "Go outside, if
you must," said the Baron who sank down among
his comrades. Someone threw him a towel and wrap-
ping it about his head, Ernie managed to get into the
corridor and hold to the wall. Inside they sang, one
voice after another, in a very slow meter, the *Horst
Wessel Lied*. "Get back to your room," said an old
caretaker moving around him in the darkness. Finally, his head white and bulky in the towel, he made
his way out into the rain, leaving a sharp odor of
sickness outside the room with a light.

Stella, golden tresses gathered about the waist, a
calm determination to survive and to succeed grown
upright in her mind, waited for his return, sure he
would come, sure she would have to give warmth.
She was prepared to make him as happy as her instinct would allow, would overrule the rights of anyone in the house for her own demands. But Gerta
was a woman quick to injure. Stella listened to every
sound, fought with the desire to dream, and thought
at some hour of the night that she heard marching
feet. When Ernie finally did come, it was in desperation. "Come in, you poor creature," she whispered,

and held the toweled bundle in her lap. He left soon after because a bright excited day was beginning to break, and harassed or jubilant cries echoed up and down the drying streets.

STELLA

The conquered spirit lies not only in rest but in waiting, crushed deep in face-lines of deprivation, in fingers that no longer toil, the one thing that shall lift, and enlarge and set free.

The house where the two sisters lived was like an old trunk covered with cracked sharkskin, heavier on top than on the bottom, sealed with iron cornices and covered with shining fins. It was like the curving dolphin's back: fat, wrinkled, hung dry above small swells and waxed bottles, hanging from a thick spike, all foam and wind gone, over many brass catches and rusty studs out in the sunshine. As a figure that breathed immense quantities of air, that shook itself in the wind flinging water down into the streets, as a figure that cracked open and drank in all a day's sunshine in one breath, it was more selfish than an old General, more secret than a nun, more monstrous than the fattest shark.

Stella combed her hair before the open window, sunlight falling across her knees, sometimes holding her head up to catch the wind, as wide awake as if she had slept soundly through the night without wild dreams. A few scattered cheers and broken shouts were carried up from side streets, windows were flung open, dust-rags flung out into the spring morning like signal flags. Brass bands were already collecting in the streets, small groups of old men surrounded by piles of shiny instruments. A crowd was gathering about the front of the gated house and she could hear them stamping their feet and clapping each other on the backs, thumping and pushing, waiting for the chance to cheer. She felt completely at rest, self-satisfied, pulling at one strand of thick hair and then at another. She knew her father would be dressing, powdering his cheeks so he could speak to the crowd, and she had reached the time of a strange discovery. If it were not for the idea of love, if her father were a man she did not know at all, how distasteful his fingers would be, like pieces of rotting wood; how unpleasant his white hair would be, a grey artificial mat that she could never stand to kiss; how like an old bone would be his hollow shoulders. Stella enjoyed thinking of her father as one she did not know. He was so old he never understood. Voices shouted at her, she eased her chair to follow the moving sunlight. Gerta came in throwing the door wide.

"Damn that woman, damn that old fool!" Gerta stared about the room. "Always I say I'm not at home, I've gone away to the country, I'm sick, but there she sits, down there with the cook in the kitchen waiting to pounce on me." The old woman raged about the room, hovered over the chair a moment to see if Stella listened. She snorted at the golden head, ripped into the closets, threw forth bundles of soiled linen. She gasped.

"You're no better!" The comb slid up and down, the nurse trembled in the pile of linen.

Down in the kitchen sat Gerta's friend, a new maid from several houses away who traveled across back courts and had paid a call, for no reason, carrying a bag of cold buns which she munched while trying to become friends with Gerta. Gerta was afraid and angry and could not understand this woman who, dressed like an imbecile girl, wore her thin hair plastered to the head, who had no name and talked forever. Gerta would not touch the buns.

"You're no better. And don't think," the voice was a whisper, distorted and low, "that I don't know what went on last night. Don't forget that!"

Her father fussed with his collar, a rouge color filling in flat cheeks, her mother directed him from beneath the sheets, the crowd screamed when a man-servant hung a faded flag from the very narrow balcony.

Stella turned, face shrouded in gold. "Get out. Take the clothes and leave." The old woman raced from the room hauling the delicate silks and wrinkled trains of cloth, stumbled and ran, and the hairbrush sailed through the door over the mammoth baluster and fell in a gentle curve to crash many floors below on the hard marble. She turned back to the light. The insurrection passed lightly as the brush, she was bounded by the pale bed, the brightening walls, and summer. The cook howled for more butter from a stuttering girl, the visitor chopped a bun. There on the floor, there beside the small proper bed was the spot, now in shade, where she had held him in her lap.

Despite the dark brown symmetry and shadows of the buildings outside, the air was filled with a light green haze. It patiently and warmly lifted itself over the sagging branches, weakened beneath the load of fresh young leaves scattered on trees caught between the walls and sidewalk. The morning with its widening haze, voices wrangling over the fences, brushes and rags fighting with the furniture, tousled girls scraping and whispering on their knees, the house filled itself with boys and tremendous baskets of fruit, hauling in, it seemed, crowds of people out of the city, awoke with cries and attention. That was the moment to sit in the sun with soft hair falling about one's waist, to doze and wake, nodding and smelling the sweet air, collecting thoughts for years to come or gone by, like an old woman hooded in black in a doorway.

A half-dozen birds, caught in the leaves, tried to make themselves heard and far down the hall she could hear Gerta talking to her father who was trying to dress. The air was like honey to wave beneath her nose; she called forth her own pleasure, plucked anywhere from the moving number of summer sensations. She waved her hand, even on the opening day of war, the public's day, and a gentle lusty swell crowded her head, shoved the half-dozen murmuring birds out of reach. In winter, the snow fell where she wished, in great dull even flakes, in smooth slightly purple walls where far in perspective she was held like a candle, warm and bright. In summer, alone, it was she that breathed the idea of naked moonlight swimming—divers together in the phosphorescent breakers, leaves as clothes on the silver beach—she that breathed the idea of brownness, smoothness into every day of June, July, August, who created hair over the shoulder and pollen in the air.

Her mother, a long mound beneath the sheets, had lost all this, terribly aged with a cold pallor, strong and indolent, unhappy in the oppressive heat. The mother lay in bed day after day, the spring, summer, years dragging by, with only her head two hands long above the sheets, her eyes fastened together, motionless until some forgotten whim, surge of strength, drove her from the bed. And in that hour she would shop. When she shopped, she ventured on the streets in gowns from another date, walked in steady steps, and took Stella along. She never liked the world she saw and her old husband never knew she was out of the house.

A hundred strokes, a hundred and five, the hair quivered in the space of gold; she changed hands, her skin as soft as the back of a feather. Her brothers, a pair of twins, fifteen-year-old soldiers dressed in stiff academy blue and trimmed in brass, walked past her open door, eyes ahead, arms in parallel motion, and she heard their miniature spurs clanking down the wide stairs. The boys never saw their parents, since the old man and woman had been the age of deaf grandparents at the time of the brothers' remarkable conception. The brothers ate and lived alone. The jingling sound hung in her ears, one of the birds had become audible, and she thought of a parakeet with long sharp nails bathing in a blue pond where the green grass swayed and the sun was orange. There was no shock in the day, but the same smothered joy crept up with the morning's trade and old flags that were unfurling along the guarded streets.

"Breakfast, breakfast!" Gerta called, wearied and harassed, from the center of the first floor lobby, lips drawn down, clutching a fist of silver, calling to wake the whole house into an even greater activity. The shabby crowd was growing restless, howling with round faces scrubbed cheery and proud, while inside the high walls the elaborate process of serving the isolated meal began. Twenty thousand feet in the sky, a sheet of wind flashed over the city cold and thin, while below, warm air rolled over the lake in the park, and swans opened their necks and damp feathers, bumping softly together in stiff confusion.

The old man, always seated first at the table, held his head high and rigid so that it trembled, pure white eyes staring and blinking from a skull like a bird's, the whole area behind the thin tissue eaten away and lost. Sometimes he ate his melon with the fork, or spoon, or knife, or pushed it with his pointed elbow so that it fell to the floor, pits and meat splashing over his black curled-up shoes. The moustache fell to his high collar in two soft sweeping strands of pale gold, his long legs were a mass of black veins. His face, narrow and long, was covered with bark and was deep scarlet, and clots of blood formed just under the glaze of fine hair; and he would fall, slipping and breaking in every part at least once a week. But each time the clots would dissolve and be churned away, down the grass-smelling passages, and he would recover.

The table was so short, with the twelve leaves piled out of sight in dust, that she could almost smell his breath, with scarcely a bare foot of candelabra, bowls, tongs, green stems and silver trays between them. When she sat down, his head, like a brittle piece of pastry, tried to swim over the breakfast things, searching as every morning, but was blocked by a twisted maze of fern in an azure vase and a pyramid of butter patties topped with dark cherries. "Stool," he said in a high voice because he could no longer pronounce her name. They sat close together in the middle of the long dining room, the man with his ninety years and the young girl with her peaches, while overhead, set in one of the domes, a large clock struck eleven. Gerta hurried in and out pushing a little cart laden with napkins, rolls, knives, sauces of all kinds and pans of under-done, clear boiled eggs. "Poor man," she said, dabbing at a long run of fresh egg water on his tunic, turning now and then a look of wrath on Stella as if the poor girl herself had shaken his freckled hand and made the long translucent string slide off onto his chest. Stella frowned back, scattering crumbs over the little table and knocking the goblet so that a mouthful of water sizzled on the coffee urn.

"Watch what you're doing," snapped Gerta, her slippers padding angrily on the rug.

This morning he was able to get the pink slices between his fingers, but, slipping through their own oily perfume, they constantly fell back to the tablecloth in irregular heaps of quivering jelly. Stella thought of Ernie and smiled across the floral table at her father, looked with delightful interest at his slippery hands.

The boy didn't realize what he said, 1870, it would take many dead men to encircle Paris, and the responsibility, that's what he didn't understand or no one could speak in such a manner, pride on the heights. "War," her father said, and there was a terrible fire in his eye through the ferns. "War," and he leaned slightly forward as if to strike her, but his arm only raised part way, shivered, and dropped back on the plate. She stopped smiling.

"Where is the railroad station?" he asked.

Stella watched his questioning face for a moment then continued to eat. She was sorry.

"He only wants to go to the bathroom," said Gerta, and throwing herself under his thin erect frame she led him out, the white lace duster fluttering on her head. The two boys clanked by in the hall, stepped in a single motion out of the way. The cook worked frantically to heat more rolls in the oven like a boiler, kept a flame under the pot of coffee, ran from cupboard to cupboard collecting more juices and spices, threw a large ham on the spit. Stella pulled the long brocaded sash and heard the bell jingle out amid the clatter of pans, the swirl of water. Gerta's friend came in, still wearing her brown shawl and hat covered with violets, still clutching the paper bag with grease on her fingers.

"More toast," said Stella.

"Ah, toast," said the woman and disappeared.

Stella thought that her father suffered very much. Some parts of the day she would walk with him up and down the beautiful quiet hallways, his hand resting only lightly on her arm, a smile about his shriveled lips. Sometimes she suffered herself, though usually in the evening in the blue shadows of her room, never in the morning, for she knew that at dusk she would see him half-hidden and in full stately dress behind the tall lighted candles. The dining room walls darkened with nightfall, the silverware lighted by the flames, the immense shadows falling over him from white flowers instead of ferns, covered him with an illusory change that frightened her. In these evenings Stella remembered how, when she was a small girl, he had talked to her, before his voice disappeared, and she heard his voice talking of sieges and courtships, and emerald lands, and she wished him to be a father still. At night she could not tell. From a few long talks with her mother she knew that for five generations the men had been tall, handsome, discreet and honorable soldiers, all looking exactly alike as brother eagles, and all these men had died young. Her father had so outlived the features of those other men and his family that he no longer existed and could not even speak. The man hidden behind the candles made her wonder for all his years.

"You don't have to tell me where he needs to go," she murmured, and Gerta's friend returning with the toast was confused by her words.

The hair nearest her neck was hazel, the rest lemon, and when she walked it was fitfully gliding as if she were already there—there in the mausoleum where he lay in plaster, where rose petals were swept under her prayer. For in the hottest part of the noon, the house was withered away and his white face was in a lasting repose, the idiot of breakfast, the marshal of dinner, become an old masked man in the heat of the sun wherever she walked. She would gladly cut the epitaph herself for just one glimpse before they latched the door—the noon heat made her feel the marble dust as if it were fresh. Never in the world could she know him, only scraps from her mother's carefully guarded chest. Sometimes, when Stella looked most beautiful, she felt that she would collapse with the house around her when he finally left.

Her room nearest the slate roof was warm, the seascapes, spaced regularly over the walls filled it with blue, the birds had become silent under the window. Jutta, an ungainly eleven-year-old child, was taking her nap at the end of the corridor in a cubicle small and low that might have belonged to a boarding school or nunnery white and bare. Her mouth was open and she breathed heavily, thin legs apart as if she were riding a horse. Stella fastened the bonnet with pink and yellow ribbons, drew on her white gloves, started down the stairs, and stopped to listen to the low ugly noises of the sleeping child. Outside she found herself caught in front of the house in the silence of the crowd, and all eyes looked upward. There on the narrow balcony, squeezed side by side, was her father still leaning on Gerta who smiled, laces fluttering against his uniform. All at once he spoke, and the single word fell upon them hushed and excited. "Victory." For a moment they waited for more, watched, listened and then broke out in screams of appreciation while the old man was led back inside the house. They did not realize that he thought the war, which had just begun, was over, and they took up the word and sent it flying along the street from one startled citizen to the next. Stella began to walk, her parasol catching the shade of the enormous line of trees.

Men tipped their hats, drays rolled by with heavy rumps nodding majestically between the shafts, chains clattering, whips stinging; small flags hung limply in shops as if it were a holiday. A tremendous stuffed fish grinned out at her, sunlight skipping between its blue fins, small clams grey and moist piled about like its own roe on the chopped ice. An awning covered part of the street with orange, passers-by parted into even chattering lanes, and children going to the park grinned, tugging ahead. In the Krupp manufacturing works, huge steel barrels were swung by chain and arm, covered with pale green grease and pointed through barred skylights towards the summer sky. In the jail, prisoners looked out into the white limestone yard, carriages skimmed by on frail rubber wheels, and lapel after lapel spotted with a white flower passed by her side. In the thrill of this first warm exciting day with posters going up all over the city and mothers proudly patting their sons' heads, Stella's aunts and uncles, less fortunate cousins and acquaintances, fanning themselves in desolate drawing rooms or writing down the date in diaries, wondered how the beginning of hostilities would affect her father's position, and donning bright colors, prepared to call.

A swallow dipped suddenly down into the center of traffic, and up again, successful. It was then that the headache began. It came as a dull burn might come in noon hours on the beach, a soft sensation in her eyes; pleated under the yellow hair, it coursed slowly down the small of her neck, and made mouthfuls of spit shimmer above the policeman's white-lady gloves. She held her hand to her breast because the headache was so tiny and almost caught in her throat. "Oh, yes," she said to herself, "I've seen so many artists," and indeed she had once passed a man slumped over a table scratching the fleas. The seascapes about the walls of her room reminded her of the warm south, of islands where the white sun hurt the eyes, of pebbles like the tips of her fingers that were pearl grey. She could never laugh at anyone, a velvet shoulder brushed quickly by, sharp blues and reds hurried along the street. "Your father was a wonderful brave loving man," her mother would say. Dogs barked and howled, she glanced from yellow walls to white, creating as she walked small impressions which remained precious and a source of continual inspiration, catching a swift dark eye of possible European fortunes, pitying the shoe with the twice normal heel. The buildings, low, gilded, with their spires thrust a ludicrously short way into the sky, all trying to fall upon the street, protected by iron spikes, cast a yellow fog against the clouds. When her face was serious, when she watched the drays or passing blurred numbers cut into stone, watched the street as it moved, when her face was vacuous, it was

a little flower, as if the larger girl had walked away
to find Father. But when she smiled the mouth was
tense, desire lost upon the waving of her arms. Gerta,
when the moon was starting to sink, used to carry
her away from the mother's bedside; and, awake with
the nursemaid guarding the door, she could hear the
old man snoring fitfully somewhere in the corridor.
The sun hurt her eyes; it was certainly more difficult
to hear now that her head hurt her so. "Your father
was a tall man and we went to the mountains before
they had railroads." When, infrequently, she talked
to her mother, she was speaking through her, as
through a black unsteady ear-trumpet, to a very old
man who sat listening, pallid in a rocking-chair, some
thirty or forty years ago. Now in his toothless eye
she was to him some rifleboy with a sack of powder
at the hip. "Victory," somebody shouted, and a boy
came running down the smoke-filled street without
his cap.

The tail end of the park was a narrow stretch of
scrubby green caught tightly between high walls in
the center of the city, an acre where the sun
rarely fell, and low office men smoked at all hours.
Strangely enough, today it was bright in the sunlight,
and there were more clerks than ever, black and limpid. Stella walked up and down between two benches
that left slat marks on shiny britches. Twisted black
toes of shoes, stuck by the loungers into the narrow
path, touched the hem of her gown, her head fluttered beneath the ribbons, pained worse, and a huge
dog with black and white spots trotted by. The sky
would darken for a moment with a smudge of cream,
then would roll back to sheer white, turning the
patches of grass to straw. Once she had hidden from
Gerta beneath her mother's skirts, had felt the over-

powering comfort of her ruffles, and that was a strange experience. The mother had thrust heavy hands under the folds, caught the wriggler, and handed the daughter over to the nurse, who always gave bad advice, to be secured in a strict manageable grasp. "Your father wouldn't like you to behave like that." Stella shut out all the city but this one pasture, shut out all the light but that which ached in her head, and high above the whispering clerks realized she loved Ernst very much. City and keeps and road-ways in the heat, he, by a forest of young hair, pro-tected from that which is dying. She waited patiently.

"My God, simpleton, why don't you sleep?" The mother spoke from a throat puffing over the edge of the sheet drawn tightly above her bosom with both hands. The father, back in the shuttered room with his tunic unbuttoned, wandered more bent and drawn around the three sides of the bed, his fine Roman nose twitching with excitement, the top of his scalp a sullen red. The room was sheltered, warm, an au-burn fuzz glowed through the shutters and darkness. The old woman was white and still in the bed and about her the black wood was inlaid with bits, broken wings, of silver. The father was in one of his reveries, counting very slowly some outlandish or important number on his yellow fingers that would never total. Though one body was heavy and the other frail, though one voice bullied and the other barely mum-bled, though the man wavered in agitation and the woman lay in state, they both were very much the same, because on both the hair had receded and be-come pale, leaving the foreheads, eyes and mouths expressionless with old age. A palmist looking at their hands would have seen no life for all the mazes of fine-drawn yellow lines, overlapping soft pads and untaken crowding roads. "If only he would slip off into the light of Heaven," she thought. "Sit down," she said, but he paid no attention, and she could hear only the long-legged rustling of his uniform, the unbearable sun pressing above them on the roof.

Jutta awoke and the room was filled with black shapes.

The heat seemed to grow more determined, even the clerks panted, whispering closely in each other's ears, and Stella believed the sun would never fall flaming through the torpid clear sky. She wondered how the strange wild cannibals on tropical islands or on the dark continent, running with white bones in their hair, dark feet hardened in the shimmering sand, could bear, in only their feathers, this terrible sun. For the headache made her drowsy. She saw those men, carrying victims high over their heads, as tall, vengeful creatures who sang madly on their secret rock, who even at night slept on glistening pink stone in fire, who stretched their tall bodies whether in repose or in chase, and who kept wives bare from the waist up. Their ears were pierced, insects buzzed low over the children, the islands kept rising up out of the sea. Even when she was tired and desperately warm and even in such a trembling state, she loved him. Her temple throbbed, the clerks were watching. Her fired heart and sweltering faith were beginning to fall away, swept by impatience. She was tired of this park filled with noise, so close to the passing horses that wore skull caps with holes for the ears. She was afraid of being left alone. Then, before she had a chance to meet the image come too sudden before her, before she had a chance to guard against this reflection which she had searched for in all the shop windows, and guard against the terror of herself, she saw him running across the street and up the path, turned half sideways, thin, excited, smiling wildly through the fresh bandages round his head.

"Stella!"

"Ernst!"

They walked for twenty minutes under the yellow and green leaves and passed the cool pond as clear as the sky, smelled the berries cultivated by the park authorities, a few beautiful dripping flowers, and passed babies who screeched, dwarfed in the carriage. Then he took her home, left her, feeling at last the approach of twilight, feeling his heart full and as vague as water.

By the end of the next week the first thousands were far into enemy land, ammunition trains roared all through the night, the city burned late in tumultuous but magnificent organization, and the house was full of callers trying to pay respects to her parents in the bedroom. All seeking on their padded feet to scale these, her walls, to climb over them in a house that was no more hers than theirs, to seek out the mother, flies over the white sheet, for knowledge of the venerable man, they crawled exactly as she crawled. She caught, unwittingly, scraps of words, part of love during the seven days and forgot about the cannibals. "We met in a beautiful copse on a summer's eve, smelling the dew." But through the hours, while Gerta stamped about serving tea to them in the anteroom, where they still wore their monstrous hats, she felt for some reason as if these short-winged creatures, all but strangers, had come to mourn, and that mourning, visiting with the dead, was the last desperate attempt, the last chance for gossip. She felt that they were taking away the joy of sunshine, casting a blot, like an unforgivable hoard, on the very search and domestic twilight peace that she did not understand. The seascapes lost their color, in the midst of this remarkable mobilization she began to feel cheated. Ernst was gone for that week, and the old house was sealed tight though they squeezed through the doors and windows. Jutta was more rude than usual.

The seventh morning was freakishly cool. All the light was gone, the fruit flat, the clatter of servants obtrusive and harsh, bands playing in the park were loud and off key. They settled down. The old man beat about the empty halls quicker than usual, the brothers whispered, the entire ring of dark chambers was gathered, not wistful but strained, unhappily into the tight present. Men were pushed first on one shoulder, then on the other, off into the grey line, and the whole house from rafters of teak to chests of wine began to shiver. That morning the mother stepped out of the bed as if alive, stared for one moment about her in the unpleasant shadows and with exact stoic movements began to dress and became, gradually, monstrously large. She was dressed in a long black gown, heavy grey gloves, a tight ruffled collar, and a hat with an enormous drooping brim that made the dark patches around her eyes and in the cheeks more prominent, more like injuries to hide. At one time, years ago, the mother had left the father and had come back three months later thin as a rail, lovely. Now her age hung upon her in unlovely touches, though she stepped out today as if to make one last effort to slough them off. Her black patches were fierce and when it was known that she was up, the house fell into silence, though the father still moved fitfully, getting in the way, as if something were wrong. The mother had somewhere forgotten about morals, self-conquest and the realm to come. She was too weighted down, it was time to go, for age filled in the lacking spaces.

Stella carried the deep basket, the streets were empty, a few luminous clouds blew hastily across the horizon beneath a smoke-black overcast thousands of feet higher. She took her mother's arm in a gesture, warmly, of confidence.

"I will have those lemons, please." The bald-headed man dropped them in, flapped his apron at a pink-nosed dog. Flies hung over the blue meat.

"Potatoes." They rolled among the lemons in dust. The silly girl spilled the money on the counter, it grew darker.

"Apples." From the trees, the branches, sprinkled with water, green leaves. The basket began to fill, the vendor limped.

Live fowl in a dirty cage were silent, claws gripping the rods caked with lime, eyes blinking at each movement.

"Melons, your father likes melons." They were scarred and green and made the basket heavier. The grocer's boy peeped out from behind a hogshead of cheese, red tongue wagging, bare feet scuffing the sawdust.

The mother and girl began to cross the street.

ERNST

Behind them one of the chickens began to scream, and a speck appeared in the sky.

"I think I must stop and buy some flowers." A few loiterers got out of their way, the old woman considered her list.

"You don't want to make yourself tired, Mother."

The day was peculiarly uninteresting, a deliberately cold day with all the summer bugs taken to cover, a few shrubs turned under and splashed dismally with a final blue, all open windows shaded, sleepers uncomfortable, a few omnibuses swaying to and fro, empty, unhurried.

"I think I'll get . . . ," said the mother, but spoke nothing more, looking with the utmost distaste upon her desolate native avenue, façades smothered with an uneven hand, scant twigs swept into the drains, not a single mortal. That was all.

The policeman's call faded into nonsense, into unutterable confusion as the speck fell quickly from the sky, two small leathered heads trapped in smoking holes, the engine, no larger than the torso of a man, blasting, whistling, coughing stupidly. It swooped over mother and girl, flapped its fins once, and crashed, typically English, on the other side of the *Platz*. Paper and wood burned quickly, consumed the flyers, leaving the isinglass still intact over their eyes. In so falling with its mechanical defect, the plane sent a splinter flying into the mother's breast that knocked her down.

The policeman kept pushing Stella by the shoulder while the half-dressed crowd asked again and again, "What happened to the old trumpet?" What happened was that they stumbled out into the street and came upon an old dead woman, kicked around, bent, black. "What are you pushing me for?" The sweet grass burned back in the passageway of the street, the old medium was so wrapped in smoke that the father's second voice, this mother, was choked, mute, with cinders in the cleft of her chin and above the open lips.

"Gavrilo," Stella murmured, "what have you done?"

The birds twittered in angelic surmise, reeled high and low, fed, nested, called beyond the curtains in gentle mockery, and the days passed by with the temperate clime of summer stones. The marble dust fell in rest; leaded curtains, lately drawn, hung padded and full across the sunlight, keepers of the room. The seascapes were gone, no shadows were on the walls, silver flukes that seemed arisen from the past hushed their soft seashell voices and at every dead night or noon, she missed the chiming of the bells. Her mourning was a cold wave, a dry flickering of fingers in departure, a gesture resting softly in her throat that barely disturbed the gentle shift of light passing on its way. It was always dusk, rising, waking, falling with indolence, resounding carefully in her sleep, reporting the solitude of each day past. Stella thought the bier was close by. That perpetual afternoon clawed about her knees, each day the spirit grew more dim, sheltered behind the heavy lost mask of falling air, the thick south receding.

Those ships that had once rolled in on the breakers were cold and thin and had traveled far beyond her sorrow. The mother's hands were crossed, the wrinkles had strangely deepened until the face was gone, the flowers were turning a cold earthen brown. Her black collar was aslant on the neck, her own mother's ring before her was tucked into a hasty satin crevice by her side, wrapped in paper. They sprinkled water about trying to keep the air fresh, and the trimmings began to tarnish. In the evening the face changed color. Sweetness arose from the little pillows; she wore no stockings or shoes and the hair, brittle and thin, clipped together, was hard to manage. The eyelids swelled and no one visited.

Stella waited, awake on the chair, listening to the hushed footsteps, her face in the constant pose of a circus boy, misshapen, cold, her isolation unmoved with memory, numb with summer. The mourning of the virgin, as if she were swept close, now, for the first time, to the mother's sagging breast for her first dance, was heightened in a smile as the orchestra rose up and they glided over the empty avenue, the old woman in starched collar leading, tripping. Those dry unyielding fingers brushed her on, poised, embarrassed by the face that never moved. She did not stop, seeing many other eyeless dancers, lured through her first impression of this season, clear and rare, but she waited, sitting, hour on hour. Those fingers rustled in the dark. She heard the perpetual scratching feet of insects who walked over the coffin lid with their blue wings, their dotted eyes, and an old bishop mumbled as he ran his fingers over the rectangle of edges closed with wax. They tried to curl the hair, but the iron was too hot and burned. Her nostrils, rather than dilated in grief, were drawn closely, dispassionately together, making two small smudges on the apex of her nose.

Sometimes she thought she had waved. She saw the ship's poop inching its way farther into the distance on the flat water, a few unrecognized faces staring back, and smelled for a moment the odor of fish. The sea rolled noiselessly away, and walking back, all the paths choked with marble dust, the air smelled of linen, of dead trees. And all Stella's forebears had finally made this journey—the ocean was filled with ships that never met. No matter how much powder they sprinkled on the mother's face the iron grey color would lie stiffly under the skin the following morning. At night they placed a lamp beside her chair, and in the first light took it away again, its flame brushing the stiff folds of her dress, shining weakly as the smooth disturbed crests of the waves, almost extinct. Each morning she sat just as straight, as if she did not know they had prowled all about her during the midnight hours, beyond the globe of the lamp. She would never see them sailing back, and this most distant visitor, lying in state nearby, asleep day and night, so changed by the assumption of the black role, seemed waiting to bring her to the land of desire, where her weeping would cover all the hill above the plain. Stella's face became gradually unwashed, her arms grew thin, the fingers stiff, her mouth dry, trying to recall this person's name. The attendants and sudden last visitors perspired. The old woman grew damp as if she fretted.

Finally they took the coffin out of the house.

On that day Ernie sat at her feet, and again it was so hot that the birds buried their heads in the shade under their wings, the fountains were covered with chalk, the room close. They heard the scuffling in the corridor and on the stairs as the coffin made its way out of the house, and the servants milled about in the lower hall, talking, weeping, holding the doors. Ernie wanted to open the curtains but did not dare.

"You don't even have a cross," he said. His beloved was silent. "You don't even have any candles, no face of Christ, no tears. What can I say?"

Then she began to murmur and he was astonished.

"I'm sorry. I will believe in the eternity of souls, I am bereaved. I will see those places where death talks solemnly to the years, where the breakers roll over their sins and their regrets, where the valley of Heaven lies before the crag of immortality, and I will believe my mother has gained peace. I have lost her. Has anyone felt such terrible grief, known that for all earthly time the eyes shall never see, the heart never beat except with her shadow? What an unhappy loss, the candles are gutted, and the face wanes for this immortality. I have lost my mother."

This was her only glimpse of Heaven, and she wept so much that he was afraid. Finally she held his hand. The two brothers fired the cannon at the burial.

That night Stella went to live in her father's room, since he could not be left alone, and he watched her with troubled suspicion as she slept, filling only half the invalid's ponderous space. She walked amid heaps of soiled nightdresses, rows of enameled pots for the old man, the stale smell of bones and flies, emptied the deep drawers of food he had hidden, awoke in the gloom and confusion of yesterday's air. She sang him lullabies well after midnight, fed him with a spoon, scrubbed the pale face and neck, fought with Gerta over his mad words, and still he could not keep alive. The odor of sweet grass again became heavy, and one morning she found him, tongue rolled under, the top of his head a brilliant swollen red, clutching a feathered helmet across his breast. She had not even awakened.

Where is the railway station?

The leaves turned heavy on the branches, birds coursed away, forgotten, and the cold chill of a new season descended on the city with rain and late fever.

The great ring of chopped ice rumbled thousands of feet below them without moving. Jagged and slender like headless flowers, like bright translucent stems, the quivering clear stalks of ice shot rays of sun back and forth over the soundless field. It was as if the hotel's foundations were buried finally so far below in this unreal brilliant bed that the sudden sensation of holiday traveled up and down the polished floors to the center of the clear colorful ice, that the wine flowed first pink and then golden in sheer chasms where little men in feathered hats filled it with song. With pick, rope, spike and red shirts they climbed in the afternoons, hung waist to waist over the most treacherous graves in Europe, and at night it snowed, or the moon rose ringed with a faint illumination in the darkness. The mornings climbed upwards from the valley in violent twists and turns, leaping from one shelf of ice to the next, turning the flat grey blades into brilliant shattering arms of light until they finally rose above the gasping mouth of the hotel in cold transparent wings of color, holding them motionless, suspended in gravity amidst an unanchored spectrum.

Stella and Ernst found themselves in the midst of healthy guests, the men giants, the women tanned with snow, even the old venerable and strong because they were not too old. A few children chased each other about the lobby and bowed when approached by adults. Their short rasping voices were small and unawares out of doors, and there was a fear that they would fall into the ice floes. "It's a great mistake," Stella said, "to think that the youngest children are the most lovely—they're not." And yet she thought these children, the sons and daughters of the straight athletes, were beautiful. She watched them romp with hostility, and yet they flowered before her, danced and played. "The younger they are the more they demand, the more helpless they are. They're capable of more than we think, especially when they can't talk." They lit their cigarettes and passed out of earshot of the children. Ernst was bundled to the throat in a jacket of bright fur and smiled and nodded at all she said, the tufts of long hair rubbing against his neck. Now that he was on the heights and all below him was gone, he walked always with spikes on the soles of his feet so he would not slip. Hearts in their hands, he slung the rope on his shoulder but never went down, for they wanted to be alone, high, in this one place. The whiteness flashed up, clearing away the last traces of summer, and Stella, looking over such a profound staged landscape, clung to his arm as if he would fall. But he was nearer God.

Every afternoon the old horse stood wheezing by the porte-cochere, trembling slightly with head lowered from the terrible exertion of the long climb. The sleigh would be empty, a rug dragging on the packed snow. The horse appeared blind, so limply hung the head, so blank the closed lids, and little drops of frost grew in his nostrils and on the bit, clung embedded in the sparse mane. He was cold, black and thin and hung with red trappings that did not fit, that swung against his damp hide with each painful bellow of air. Stella always tried to feed a piece of sugar to the flabby lips and slime-covered steel, but always the dumb groping nose knocked it from her palm. "Ah, the poor beast," Ernst would say, looking over the sucked-in tail and fragile hocks. "You could count his age on all the ribs." Then the driver would come out, sinister eyes rolling over his muffler, followed by the departing families with their skis. The black horse stumbled down the hill, and the couple continued their honeymoon, two golden figures in the setting sun.

Behind those flat drooping lids, the horse's eyes were colorless and strangely out of shape, but they were deep, shy, inhumanly penetrating. The knees shivered both backwards and forwards.

This was the upper world. Some of the guests whisked in the morning down to the lower and with each sharp descent in the process, the pitch of their enjoyment dropped, until it was too low to bear. And quickly as possible, they laboriously began the crawl back upwards to the clear air, waiting to laugh until they had reached the point where they could turn and let their eyes glide down in cool recreation over those falling fields. The upper world was superior. In the lower, tufts of grass poked dangerously through the snow; snarling dogs ran under foot; the snow turned to rain on the lowest fields, and the isolated huts were grey and sodden. The laughter was above, the easiness that was tense with pleasure, the newness poured itself over the winged guests in

85

sudden, unexpected delight, for a few days or weeks. The cooking was excellent. The black horse thrived better in the lower world. He was the same horse the students rode, shivering with the cold, tied alone to suffer the night. And yet he carried them, their switches flicking in the wind.

Here in this beautiful forest of burnt furniture, amidst the pale coolness of the wide-flung windows, in the crackling of parlor fires, in the songs beyond the thick rustic walls and the love inside, it did not matter that Herman said he was sorry to see her go, that the *Sportswelt* would miss her. The remembrance of the old house and the old parents, her sister, Jutta, was a far-off thing.

The hotel, from its highest porch where Ernie hid himself to watch all those who approached, to its gradually widening foundations where the mountain flowers shriveled and curled against the stone, was the center of a small acre of snow-packed land, was the final peak of a mountain. During the long rail trip they had watched the winter arrive, the smoke from squat chimneys more grey and thick. The snow fell, first in warning flurries, settling more coldly on the weaving branches and huddled animals. Winter was near the hotel.

At the far end of the acre was a small house, the roof curling under a foot of snow, its rear window gazing outward twenty miles and downwards to the depth of a thousand feet. Stella and Ernst, holding hands, silent in wondrous amazement, turning and clapping each other in excitement, walked over this very acre every afternoon and passed the house. A few scrubby trees leaned dangerously over the cliffs. And every afternoon they passed the old man on the doorstep, brittle shavings heaped over his shoes and like yellow flakes blown on the snow. He grinned while he carved, looked up at them, seemed to laugh, and hunching his shoulder, pointed backwards, behind the hut, out into the emptiness. The crosses he carved were both small and large, rough and delicate, some of simple majesty, others speaking minutely of martyrdom. They too fell across his feet, mingled with the sticks of uncarved wood—sometimes a bit of green bark was left to make a loincloth for Christ. Those that were not sold hung inside from a knotted wire, and slowly turned black with the grease and smoke; but the hair was always blacker than the bodies, the eyes always shone whereas the flesh was dull. Tourists paid well for these figures that were usually more human than holy, more pained than miraculous. Up went the shoulder, the knife rested, and he was pointing to the nearness of the cliffs. After the first week, Ernie bought one of the crucifixes, a terrible little demon with bitter pain curling about the mouth no larger than a bead, drawing tight the small outward-turning hands. Then he began to collect them, and every afternoon a new Christ would peer from his pocket through the tufts of fur.

By now his prayers at mealtime were quite audible. The setting sun stained the imperfect windows, made whorls crimson and shot the narrow panes with streaks of yellow until an off-color amber, like cheesecloth, finally smeared them over and gave way to a dismal night. Chairs scuffed in unison as the five long tables filled, and in the first silence, before strange conversations were resumed, before they had recaptured their half-intimate words, while they were still only nodding or whispering, one of the tables would become conscious of an impersonal, pious mumbling. Busily rearranging the silver and china before him, his brow wrinkled, he talked as if to an old friend. The table would be hushed and uneasy until he looked up. The hotel manager, who took this time of the evening meal to appear before his gathered guests and walk up and down between the rows to interrupt a conversation or a draught of wine, was struck dumb with the unnatural monotone, and would cast significant glances at Stella. The lines of beautiful cloths, the habits of silk, the evening dress of others turned inwards upon her, incongruous with the thick china and bare walls and floor, modern and glittering and presumptuous. She touched his hand, but it was stiff and cold, smooth and pious. She thought at first that she could feel something of his Bishop's creed and was part of this furtive ritual that exerted itself more and more, even when the evenings were rich with color.

The crucifixes began to fill the hotel.

Ernst had filled their two rooms with flowers and stones, small misshapen petals that were bright and petrified, delicate and warped with the mountain air, clear opal stones polished with ages of ice. At night before they slept he arranged the flowers in her hair, and with a kiss laid her away. In the morning he would climb to the porch and spend an hour noting carefully who arrived. And he did the same in the afternoon, breathing deeply, peering intently. He and his wife were very happy. An old count nodded to them in the corridor just beginning to grow light; they awoke blushing and warm holding the covers tight with a childish guilt, and below their window the children laughed, danced and clapped. He no longer thought of the Baron, or Herman, or the *Sportswelt,* no longer thought of Stella's singing and particularly did not want to hear her sing. The altitude made him faint, he breathed heavily, and could not stand to think of pain. If anyone twisted an ankle, or if one of the children skinned a knee, or an old woman ached in the chest, he rushed to be by their side, he "stood over them," as he called it. Then the old man, the Christ-carver, began to visit the hotel regularly, bringing with him each day a basket of those crucifixes that he could not sell, so that the black ugly Christs hung upon the walls of their rooms along with the bright new ones. Children were soon seen playing with wooden crosses, lining them up in the snow, leaving them all about the playroom. A small crown prince possessed one with beautifully flexed muscles and a rough beard. Stella began to have him lean on her arm as they walked and knew that the most beautiful bird holds tightest before flying straight upwards.

It was almost is if the whole family lived in the next room, asleep in the pile of trunks under the hanging window. The trunks collected dust and beneath the arched lids one of her mother's gowns slept with Herman's waistcoat, a militant comb lay straight and firm by a yellow brush. A pair of medical tweezers that had plucked the fine moustache grew old near one of Herman's mugs. The trunks were sealed with wax. All together they were happy, and a flute player charmed the two rooms.

On a morning in the third week Ernst left her side and climbed to the porch. Above the snow there was light, but the thick flakes, like winter, covered all the mountaintop in darkness, beat against his eyes, swept over his knuckles hooked to the railing. He watched. It was impossible to see where the acre ended and where the deep space began, the fall. He waited, peering quickly, expecting the messenger, sure of the dark journey. "Look over the plains," he thought, "and you will see no light. No figures, no men, no birds, and yet He waits above the vast sea. Thine enemy will come, sweeping old ties together, bright as the moon."

Ernst had given up the sword; though his wounds were healed, the Heavens gaped, and he had lost the thread of the war's virus. Then, at the bottom of the flurry, he heard the arrival. The horse's bells rang as if he had been standing there, just below, all during the night and the snow and had just come to life. He heard the muffled knock of a hoof, a door slammed. A sleepy-eyed boy, his tongue still flat along his lower jaw, weaved back and forth in the wind, nearly fell beneath the bag that weighed of gold. The driver beat his gloves and pocketed the *Pfennig,* the snow raced. Ernie closed his mouth and saw through the white roof of the passenger's descent. Cromwell ran up the steps and rang the sharp bell that awoke the clerk. By the time Ernst was back in the room, bending over her in the darkness, cold and afraid, it had stopped snowing. The black horse shook off his coat of white.

Still one could not see beyond the fortress of the hotel, beyond the drops of mustard gas and mountain vapors, beyond the day that was only half risen. The children became thin and tired and the adults suddenly were unable to find their own among the solemn faces. With that sharp cry of mother to child, the parents searched among the idle play groups as if through obligation. During the three meals the tables were half empty and a great many plates were broken, as the child bites and the young mother is still forced to feed. All of them smelled the fog, it curled about their hair and chilled them in the bath, and the nurse's playing fingers could do nothing to help, while the air became more thin and the water difficult to pump.

Ernst had become more and more used to the lover's mystery, had learned timidly what strange contortions the honeymoon demands, and she, not he, was the soldier, luring him on against the fence, under the thicket, forcing him down the back road through the evening. He watched her sleep. But now it was painful, it was cold, the snow was already too thin to hide him. He walked up and down the room, could see nothing from the window because he was too near the light, and the early morning, without the hands of the clock or the morning paper, his own time, was about to break. He was already one of the cold bodies down on the ice, he felt the terrible rush of air. After pausing a moment he ran quickly down the stairs, seeing all of them dragged into the university, kicking, clawing, hunched up like camels in the dust, caught and beaten. Someone put both hands on his knees.

No one stirred, the clerk and boy were curled up to sleep again until the real morning came. The lobby was filled with cold shadows, uncollected cups, a discarded shirt, a bucket with a thin edge of ice over the top. For the first time Ernst felt that the windows were closed, the wires cut, and felt the strange sensation that the mountain was moving, tearing all the pipes from the frozen ground, sliding over unmapped places. A magazine was several months old, an electric fan turned from side to side though the blades were still.

He forced himself to speak. "How was your trip?" The man stood up, still in evening dress, smiling with the old natural grace, and he felt the fingers take his own. "Well, Heavens, to think we'd meet again. And, congratulations, you've got my admiration, she's a delightful girl." They sat together, vaguely conscious of the damp air. "I thought I was coming to a place quite different, no familiar faces, a place of rest, but it's more as if I were home. Well, you must tell me all about yourself." No one stirred. They drank the thick black coffee which Cromwell had heated himself, careful not to soil his white cuffs, while he watched the briefcase. The windows were folded in white, the hat and gloves and cane lay by the coffee pot, the heavy cane close at hand.

Gradually Ernst's head began to lean forward, closer to the table. He had told their story, they were happy, he thought someone moved overhead, but then he knew he heard nothing. Cromwell was telling him everything he did not want to know, and he waited for the footsteps of the cook or the old man or a nurse come to heat the bottles. Cromwell lectured, smiled, and spoke confidentially, with ease, about the lower world. Behind the column of figures, the sweeping statements, the old friendship there was the clicking needle, the voice coming from inside the briefcase—with facts and sieges memorized, hopes turned to demands, speaking to convince them all, from the general to the dandy. Ernst's head touched the table. Cromwell was not tired from the long ride up the mountain but spoke quickly, as if he had been everywhere and carried near his breast the delicate maps and computations, the very secrets they lived on.

". . . Antwerp fell. The Krupp gun, 42 centimeter, took them through and luckily enough, I was able to see the whole thing. It was like Hohenlohe's progress in Africa, more, you see, than just a concentration of men for their own good, more than anything like a unity of states, like the Zolleverein, rather complete success, a mass move greater than a nation, a more pure success than Prussia's in the Schleswig-Holstein affair. We fought, gained in the area of Soissons and they couldn't drive us from Saint Mihiel—glory be to the German army! The line is now from the English Channel to Switzerland, and we wait only spring. We extend across Europe in four hundred integrated miles."

It was now dark, morning turned backwards in exasperating treachery. Cold porridge was left on the table. He thought he should perhaps shake Cromwell's hand again, go fetch more coffee. He had lost the thread, the long chain of virus that keeps a man anchored to his nation, instrumental in its politics, radiant in its victory, and dead in its defeat; had lost the meaning of sacrifice, siege, espionage, death, social democracy or militant monarchism. He was lost, the newspapers scattered over the vertical cliffs, the wires coiled, cut in the snow. And he prayed at meals, knowing nothing about the collective struggle of the hated Prussian and genius Hun, knowing nothing of the encircling world, the handcuff, the blockade. That air seeping visibly below the window, through orchard and burrowed haystack, crawled by the red and yellow wires, kissed the worried *Oberleutnant,* and the dumb sapper smoking his pipe in the hole. Eyes burned; it left patches in the lungs amid the blowing of whistles, this yellow fog. It came in the window, the mountain slid lower, railway tracks giving way to on-sloughing feet.

"They are well trained," said Cromwell, "in spring, the valleys will fall under—extension—we must have technological extension. No nation has the history of ours." There was a list of seven hundred plants in his briefcase, where locomotives swung on turn-tables and the smell of cordite hovered over low brick buildings. The world is measured by the rise and fall of this empire.

The hotel manager was shaving and soon would come downstairs. A nurse, ruddy and young, behaved like a mother, smiling at the child in the darkness. In the neighborhood of Cambrai where an Allied flank-ing movement had failed to turn the German ex-treme right, a farmhouse at a fork in the clay roads, demolished by artillery fire, lay half-covered in leaves and snow. There the Merchant, without thoughts of trade, dressed only in grey, still fat, had died on his first day at the front and was wedged, standing up-right, between two beams, his face knocked back-wards, angry, disturbed. In his open mouth there rested a large cocoon, protruding and white, which moved sometimes as if it were alive. The trousers, dropped about his ankles, were filled with rust and tufts of hair.

When Stella awoke, she was still possessed of the dream; it lingered on in the dim light. When she looked into Ernst's bed, she saw only a small black-haired Christ on the pillow, eyes wide and still, who trembled, and with one thin arm, motioned her away.

"Maman," a child's voice cried below the window, "the old horse is dead!"

LUST

All night long, despite the rattle of the train wheels
and the wind banging against the loose window-
panes, Ernst could hear the howling of the dogs out
in the passing fields and by the rails. The robe hung
over his shoulders and was clutched about his throat,
the heavy folds coarse and dark, stamped with the
company's seal as railroad property. Robes were
piled in all the empty compartments, the dim light
swayed overhead, and the cold grew so severe that
the conductor, who continually wished to see their
papers, was irritable, officious. The compartment, or
salon, a public beige color, unkempt, with its green
shades and narrow seats, heaved to and fro, tossing
the unshaded bulb in circles, rattling their baggage
piled near the thin door. Those were certainly dogs
that howled. His face pressed against the glass, Ernst
heard the cantering of their feet, the yelps and panting that came between the howls. For unlike the
monumental dogs found in the land of the tumbleweed, glorified for their private melancholy and lazy
high song, always seen resting on their haunches,
resting and baying, these dogs ran with the train,
nipped at the tie rods, snapped at the lantern from
the caboose, and carrying on conversation with the
running wheels, begged to be let into the common
parlor. They would lap a platter of milk or a bone
that appeared dry and scraped to the human eye
without soiling the well-worn corridors of rug, and

under the green light they would not chew the periodicals or claw the conductor's heels. As paying passengers, they would eat and doze and leap finally back from the unguarded open platforms between cars into the night and the pack.

A small steam pipe, its gilt long flaked with soot, bent like an elbow, began to rattle and gasp, but after a few more knocks, a few more whistles from the engine straining at the head of the train, it died. The official ticketed odor of dust and stuffing, the chill around the dark ceiling of cobwebs increased, and Stella tried to rest while Ernst watched the night pass by, annoyingly slow and too dark to see. The firebox in the engine was small, wrapped up, steady and dispassionate for the night, the fireman nodded over his shovel, an old soldier moved abjectly about the empty baggage car, and Ernie, holding the shawl, wondered what terrible illness was falling on his shoulders. And all he had to show was the castoff crucifixion of a half-wit, wrapped in brown paper in the bottom of the carpetbag. They stopped at many small stations and crossings during the night, but no passengers boarded or left the train.

The honeymoon was over, the mountain far behind, and as they had begun walking down the road, the old horse long dead, Cromwell called, "Well, we'll meet soon again, sorry you have to rush," and waved awkwardly with his briefcase. "I don't think so," said Ernst, and dug his pike into the snow. There was no one, no one; they traveled alone except for the dogs over the snow whose edge, leagues beyond, was besieged. But when, the following morning, they drew into the city, into *das Grab,* hundreds of people milled about the shed, pushed near the train but paid it no attention. When she helped him down the iron steps, her face red with the frost, he knew things had changed, that the dogs had beaten them to the destination. That train would certainly never run again, he felt sure, and he knew that its journey was over. The engineer's black face was still asleep, a mailed fist caught on the whistle cord, head propped on an arm in the small unglassed window. "Fare well," said Ernst as he stepped off into the crowd that steamed and rattled like stacks and shovels and feet clattering in the bunkers.

Engines that had just arrived stood on sidings unattended, steaming, damp, patches of ice stretched over the cabs, waiting where the crews had left them, unaccounted for, unfueled. The crowd milled around wooden cars, valises were lost; returning soldiers, unmet, ran towards strangers, laughing, then backed away in other directions. The streets beyond the station were filled with unidentified men who had lost brass buttons and insignia to bands of children. Some soldiers that were carried on stretchers by medical men, waved empty cups or dozed in the shade of awnings, while their bearers drank inside. Some were seasick as they slid along under the towering gangs, bruised by trailing wagon chains, swept by the rough skirts of coats, tossed close to the crowded surface of the concourse. The streets were as close as the sliding dark hold of a prison ship, and since the continuous falling-off of arms and spirit, since the retreat, provided little fare for the dogs that beat the train. They couldn't support the town dogs and certainly not these soldiers.

Stella had carried the bags ever since leaving the mountain, and used to them by now, thin leather sides stamped with the black permits, bulging with nightshirts and a few mementos, she walked along by his side, stepped over the stretchers and stayed as close as possible without any trouble. Ernst had grown stronger during the night, he felt the air sailing past the train; all of them grew stronger as they neared the city, *das Grab*. It looked quite different, not at all as he had expected, not dark and safe and tiring in the middle of the earth, but cold and wide, packed with the confused homecomers, knapsacks filled with the last souvenirs. There were no bugs or insects, no still drooping beaks and shapeless wings on the marble walls. But crowds in front of empty shop windows and endless white platoons formed and re-formed behind the courthouse. Names and numbers and greetings were shunted between rows of bright bleak buildings and they kissed, changed dressings, in the middle of the street.

Ernst began to look for Herman. He didn't want to look for the old man, conscripted father, but felt, as a citizen, that the *soldat* should be met. He looked under the blankets, in the wagons, scrutinized the ranks, walked faster and faster but did not find Herr Snow.

"Ernst, my dear husband, wait, aren't we going in the wrong direction?"

"Where would you expect to find him, except in this way? All soldiers come here and go in this direction."

Every half-hour the trains slowed to a stop in the stockyards, tired brakemen swung to the ground while troops hurried from the cars; each half-hour the streets were more filled with tattered capes and swinging arms, and musette bags and boxes left forgotten on corners. All the soldiers appeared to think that someone was meeting them, and smoking their first cigarettes, hand grenades still in their belts, they appeared to enjoy searching, at least for a while. In any other place but *das Grab* they would not be so joyous. The musicians who had played at the *Sportswelt* were gathered about an upper window of an empty room and soldiers nearing from the distance heard the tune, caught it, sang it until they passed, and then forgot it. There was at that one place before the window some music. Ernst looked a long while for his father, leading Stella halfway around the city before they finally reached the house.

Beyond the outskirts of the grave, beyond the locked barns at the edge of town, beyond the open doorways and colored stock—out past those hundred miles of fields and cow sheds where old Herman had met his fill and lost his supper in the ditch—out past those last outposts and signal stations, far out to sea, the American Blockade turned first one way and then another in the fog. A few more crates and a barrel and orange or two sank away in the foam. There was no noise in this well-organized blockade field except the cold sound of the waves and the slapping of an oar, locks outward, against the blue tide.

Evidently Gerta was out and the house was empty. Stella, weary of the cold and the long march, glad to keep their voices, questions, and songs away from the day of homecoming, let the door sag-to past the sleeping sentry and, lantern in hand, helped her returning husband up the wide dark stairs. While the trench mortars out of town approached and stopped, then continued on, she felt his small burning cheek and, stooping, unbuttoned his fluttering shirt.

Gerta trudged with her thin legs cold among the boys, her wig tied on with a yellow ribbon, her skirt caught up at her black and blue hip, an old ungracious trollop, a soldier's girl. She would have nothing to do with the blind ones, they frightened her. But she'd met a boy the day before and dried his dressing, sang to keep up her spirits while pushing another along in his red box. She was hurried along, talking in a loud voice, in the throng, now and then her hand falling on a damp shoulder or into a loose pocket. The red box rattled on its cart wheels, bandages turned grey with coal dust, whistles called from the tangled depot, and soaked oranges sank slowly through the ocean's thick current. The pockets, she found, contained only the photographs of the deceased.

Two days after arrival, each trainload of men, smiles gone, hair long, found themselves foodless and the tin pans banged at their belts, the queues turned away. But as each group became hungry and camped on the doorsteps, a new load arrived, singing, watching, laughing, waiting to be met. The new laughers filtered through the despondent men; shops were empty but hung with new regimental flags, and as the laughers became, in turn, pale and confused, as last loaves were eaten and crusts lost, more laughers filtered in, singing, pushing, looking about *das Grab* for the first time. Gerta bumped from one to another, laughed, was carried up and down among the *krank* and lost, among the able but gaunt, among the young or bald. No one who walked these connected streets was old; the aged had been blown indoors. Suddenly the *Sportswelt* loomed ahead.

"Try this, try this, try this," she cried, and rifle butts were pitted against the sealed door, a window broke like the breast of a glass doll. They entered the place, weak and shouting, while the blonde trollop found her way out back to catch her breath.

The corridor made by the rock walls down to the

open latrine, was filled with wind-blown pieces of paper, and across the walls the tables were overturned, the lawns long and the valor-petals dry. Returning from the pea-green pit of stench Gerta almost stumbled where the Merchant fell, cocoon in his mouth, beams on his chest, months before. Her wooden shoes clicked on the green stones, skirts swung from the sides of her sharp hips. Gerta took a cigarette from a tin box hidden in her blouse, the smoke trailed into the garden and over the dead leaves.

The family was all dead. The Father, the victor, with a cocked hat and pot, had long ago wished her well. The Mother lay in the cold bunker of the street, cinders falling over the rough chin. The Sons, no longer to be with Nanny, having no longer spurs to tinkle against their boots since spurs were always removed before the body was interred, had never been parted and both lay under the wet surface of the same western road. So now alone, she wore her skirts above her knees and her bright lopsided lips were red with the glistening static day of *das Grab;* for she had survived and hunted now with the pack.

The blonde, the old nursemaid, pinched her cigarette and went back to the hall. The vandals, with tunics itching on bare chests, with packs paining and eyes red, with rifles still riding strapped to packs, searched, pawed over the dust, sat leaning against the rafters and waited. They seemed to think the orchestra would pick up, the lights flare on; they waited for the singer. The chairs were not made to sit on, the tables were against the walls, and the dust, lately stirred and tossed in the cold light, settled on the darkening planks. A cat called from one of the upstairs empty bedrooms and disappeared. Several white shoes, chair legs, hands, scraped against grey puttees. These were not looters who carried swag on their shoulders and trinkets in their arms, they did not scrounge and run. They searched as if for something in particular, walked softly about the bare room. The girls were gone with the *Schnapps*. The soldiers crowded together, tossed a few periodicals and lists of the dead, to the middle of the stage, and walked up and down the green carpet while the wheels rolled against the snow. They were now taught methodically to meet the train with blistering paws, and iodine stained their green cuffs.

Gerta laughed as she leaned close to an old hatless soldier who dozed far back in the chair, head to one side, shoulders caught against the rungs. His red beard was clipped unevenly, his wedding ring, tight about a dirty finger, was green. His nails were chewed like those of a young girl. His discharge papers rose out of his upper pocket blue and torn, and the paper disks hanging near his throat turned from red to black in the changing light. She touched his knee.

"Captain, have you a match?"

The eyes opened, the lips were moistened, they shut.

"No." The answer came in low bar-owner's German. He folded his thick hands together and slept.

"Have you come home to be rude to a lady?"

A shawl was miraculously unearthed from a bare corner, the black beads hung over a soldier's back. Cold air swept about the walls.

Slowly, eyes still shut, the big man's hand moved towards a pocket, the weight shifted slightly, the hand went deeper, the face was unshaven, dark, still passive. With another movement, he emptied his pocket on the table, the hand dropped back to his side and did not swing, but hung straight and unmoving. Among the dull coins, the knife, the tube of ointment, the cerulean clipping, the bits of wire, Gerta found a match and flicking it beneath the table, cursed and broke its head for being damp.

Children were looking in at the windows, watched with glee the Madame, matron and the uniformed Herr Snow.

"Was it a long journey, Captain?"

"Across the road, over there." She leaned closer to see.

When Gerta was kissed, she clung to his shoulders and looking over towards the light, saw the child's face. It pointed, laughed and jumped out of view. And old Herman, fully awake, touched the soft fur with his mouth and felt the wings through the cotton dress, while in the far end of town a brigade of men passed shallow buckets of water to quench a small fire. Herr Snow did not recognize the *Sportswelt* and did not know that he was kissing Stella's nurse. A rough golden forelock brushed his cheek.

Then old Snow stopped kissing, and for a moment his lips worked uneasily with no desire to speak, and he leaned back, his rough chin raised higher than the blunt nose. He smelled the breath of unsweetened soap, the odor of the comb issued by the government, and all about him were the grey backs, the crackling shoes, the children whose dead brothers were from his own regiment. Old Snow, sitting with a friend he'd never met in the *Sportswelt* he no longer knew, with small bright bugs still pestering his legs, had no right to be tired, no more right to look torn and drab than all the rest. For though he could not remember, bare shell of a man, his eyes and face wore the look on one who knows where he is going

—size without substance his expression was yet determined. It was the determination on those ugly features, the fact that he took a stand in the consideration of his own fate, that made him contemptible, that marked him as second rate, only a novice at the business of being a civil servant.

When he laughed it was the last laugh, and his whole mouth quivered as if the paper lips had been touched with feathers. Gerta laughed, but quickly, and looked through his belongings on the table once more. His once black shining boots, once steel padded and reinforced, once scorching in the sun, were now down on one side, scraped and shredded with long bare patches between the seams; tufts of mud and grass stuck to and raised the heels so that the squat man rolled as he walked on the city streets but sank and plodded in the valiant fields. A civil employee must not sink and plod.

"It's a good thing we met . . .," her mouth torn between desires, "it certainly is." She pulled back, stole a glance at the darkening windows, looked down at her thin hands. Somehow the woman, a little more sallow, a little more old, felt herself more than lightly touched. All the preceding boys she couldn't count, all the brilliant days with the city filling every hour with friends, friends, their sudden departure from the dark cold working hours, all this gaiety, the train arrivals sprinkled with glittering medals and redcross flags. All of it was brilliant and time consuming. But meeting the red-bearded man was a little different. She thought he was different and he was, with his sunken chest; he was, with his palsied fingers; he was, with his short hair shaved for medical reasons. But most of all because he had a sense that the stiff-marching, girl-getting fight was out of him. Now it was time for the father to have the son take over, time for the new horse, the milk-fed horse, to take the reins and buck, to trot up the mountain that was now too steep, the going too difficult with the snow. But Herman didn't know he had a son named Ernst, and there was no new horse, only time to try once again. Old Snow would try and try, sinking downwards in a landslide of age that would never end, until in the night, near the death of his son, he would try once more and fail.

"Come now," she said, "aren't you going to bring me close?" While the laughter faded from her voice and it wheezed, the old man seized her in the darkness and was neither surprised nor disappointed to find that there was almost nothing there.

There were no lights in the *Sportswelt*. For a long while, the old patriots were silent, the vandals and depressed soldiers about them were silent, telling stories in hushed voices, readying themselves for sleep on the great hall floor. The children were gone. And then a lone policeman on patrol, his spiked helmet dull and gleaming in the pale moonlight, himself short and thin, defenseless but warmed with beer, stood on a box and flashed his torch into the *Sportswelt* depths.

"My Lord," Old Snow realized by the light of the torch, "she has black stockings on her legs," and they were stretched, thin and taut, across his broad useless lap.

The tremendous scroll letters, so thick and difficult to read, blurring and merging and falling off in the darkness, profuse and graceless on the ornate pine walls, advertising inns that were dark, posts no longer to be filled, tours that no longer existed, plays that were done, loomed outmoded and intricate overhead as they passed in the street. Gerta pulled him along, curls slightly askew, pushing, holding back, intent upon guiding the soft cumbersome elbow. The street, partially emptied of his comrades, twisted fluidly and darkly ahead, an inopportune channel, street of thieves. Tenaciously she drew him on between the banks, led him down into the gathering arches, and for a moment old Herman saw his brother's barge, and on the pillows in the stern a gross unrecognizable female who kept him in tow on the warm musky evenings. He smelled the oil on the water and the powder sprinkled lightly on her pink curls.

"Wait, *Liebling*, please, not here on the corner, just wait a moment, only a moment." Nevertheless Gerta was flattered and this momentary flicker of life raised, deep within her, very false hopes.

He forgot the barge, but the smell of the sea lingered on until they stood before the sharkskin house, larger, darker, more out of date, more boarded up, than ever.

Within the whitewashed walls of the *Saint Glauze* nunnery, a figure, held mesmerized by the four uneven corners, gazed ruefully about her cell's inner haven. Jutta sat upon the cot's unbleached single sheet, hearing from below the tinkle of bells and creak of leather where the sisters walked around and around in precise timeless honor of the evening prayer. The veils were heavy over the young girl's face, they smelled of linen and were not scented with the fresh new rose, did not smell of the garden or heavenly pine or oil-softened hands. They had been laid on quickly and protectively, after the face was washed. The birds and squirrels were thin near the nunnery, theirs was only the fare of rain and prey of lower insects; the high walls were old and bare. She heard the women rustling unevenly in line, heard the soft devout invocation of Superior who was the only one to speak. From down below in Superior's room she heard the occasional stamping of the *Oberleutnant's* boots. She knew that he was standing straight and tall by the narrow window, smiling, patient, watching the revolution of the humble ring. Now and again she heard his voice.

"Now, Superior," he would say in his unnatural tones, "it is time again to invoke the Heavenly Father's love for our men in the field. Battery C is in a difficult position, you know." And the Mother's voice would intone once more. The *Oberleutnant* had recently been relieved of active duty and given the political position of director at the nunnery where he improved the routine and spirit a good deal. He walked fretfully himself in the garden when the nuns were asleep, at their frugal meals, or at their indoor prayers. Jutta, the young girl, imagined him directing the almost perfect prayers of Superior, could see the old woman glancing out of the tight crowded ring at the man's face hidden deep in the recess. A supply officer, he was secretly included in the older sisters' prayers, and when he walked, bent with rank and tension, he gave the impression of deep concern and all knew he was worried about the welfare of Battery C.

With the old man dead, her mother dead, her two young brothers lost to the Fatherland and her sister Stella gone to marry in the mountains, Jutta was left alone while the city was gradually corrupted into war. It was Gerta, in the last days before her flaming debauch, who took her in long arms and presented her, with reverence, to the nuns. And after the family was no more, swept into the great abyss by the ancestral tide, and Gerta had no more chores, nothing but red paint and the empty house, her friend with the buns sent a note of sympathy trimmed in black. But by the time it arrived, Gerta was on the street and it remained in the leaking mailbox with all the other dead unopened letters. After that the postman stopped calling and the old house shrank tighter, where once the Grand Duke came to call. The street fell into ruin.

One by one she heard the feet shuffling through the gravel to the sanctum door, and as each stooped woman entered into the darkness of a century of peace, the sounds in the garden stilled. The circle unwound until the sisters of charity were no more and she could hear only the *Oberleutnant* humming as he paced rapidly back and forth, replacing the characteristic tone with heresy and haste. Not a bird sang anywhere, but a small bell jangled the sisters to board and thanksgiving. Their prayers for the evening meal echoed through the damp plaster corridors and up to her unmolested cell.

Jutta remembered the ladies in plumed hats and velvet gowns with distaste, remembered Stella's sailing around the ballroom with malice, and the thought of her dead parents, so many years too old, left her unfeeling. The old memories came but briefly, as brief as the desire to own anything or to own the black trousers, and when they did come, she summoned down her pride to fight the witchery.

She heard the soup spoons in the bowls, the soldier's quick steps.

The black skirts were held down about her ankles by long thin arms, frail from the disease that calmly ate at the calcium in her bones and drank the humbleness out of her system. As yet she did not know that her brothers had died howling in retreat, and for herself, all of them could go that way. The half-hours went by and the sky grew cerulean, the ointment was under the pillow but she couldn't reach it. She leaned forward, head over the knees, and it took all this effort at balance to keep from toppling over in a black heap. With ankles now as thin as wrists, the disease was cutting deeper, and there was no one to sit her up again if she fell. So she sat as still as she could, her thin fingers clamped firmly with effort.

Her father, the old general, in the days when he could talk and she could sit on his knee, wanted her in the civil offices. But from the first, she was determinedly an architect, she built towers with blocks and barns of paper, built them where they could hardly stand on the thick rugs, built them with childlike persistence; and the smile of completion was always one of achievement rather than pleasure. As she grew older she did not smile at all and hid her queer angles and structures in her little whitewashed room, grew more and more serious, objected rationally to the public documents and taxpayer's history fostered on her by the old general. Carefully she designed herself inwards, away from the laughing women, closeshaven men, away from tedious public obligation, until she was finally accepted, one steaming afternoon, into the Academy of Architecture.

It was almost time for Superior to start her rounds, to observe, to praise and to condemn the girls who were bad physically or bad spiritually. Superior would stand in the doorway with her face that was neither a man's nor a woman's, blocking out the last bit of light with her stiff fan-like hood and robes. With her steel spectacles, pink face and sharp black eyes, Jutta thought of her as the doctor who walked so slowly and stayed, while probing, such a long while. Down below she heard the *Oberleutnant* sit heavily on one of the benches and from down the hall came the sound of an old woman putting Superior's desk in order. While no one in the city even knew the date or what was taking place, knew neither of the blockade at sea nor of the battles in the empty forests, Superior did. Every morning, after her consultations, she sat at her desk composing, in tiny script, a long laborious letter of protestation to the President of the United States. She objected to the starvation and spreading illness. It grew dark, and Jutta could not move to light the candle.

In the Academy Jutta often saw the young men lined up with their brown torsos and tight grey gymnasium trousers. At first they often smiled at her in the cold corridors and looked over her shoulder at the drawing board. But all of them now, as far as she knew, had swords and spurs like her brothers. Winning the favor of her professors, she did not have to force herself to look at them. They passed out of reach and a long line of nurseries and fortresses took their place. Besides devising a new triumphal arch and scraping hard pencils on her sanding block, she studied history. Volume after volume passed under her close disciplined study. She knew all of the Hapsburgs, knew that the Austrians and Germans were all one blood, knew that the light and life was in the East. Her fits of temper were gone, the sabers were no longer within range, but were only of use, like her brothers, in the fields far away.

Superior was coming up the worn stairs, the *Ober-leutnant,* back in his room, stepped out of his trousers. Jutta felt weaker, more weak than ever before, and down in the city the policeman put away his torch and left his beat to go to sleep.

Her remaining isolation had been debased. The General couldn't talk, the mother was absurd in his unmade bed, Stella flew off again and again until she finally met the one with the puckered face and flew for good. There was no one to give clear-headed praise, no one to admire or respect her diagrams of mechanical exultation, no one to recognize, even at thirteen, her great skill. But it was not the language of the dumb, the old, that made the declining days a treachery and not a triumph, not the dead in the streets and silence in the house that drove her to the nuns.

The final blot against absolution, depriving her of sacrifice and intelligent suffering, was Gerta's unpleasant love. When the sores first came and she fell with dizzy spells, the old fool of a nurse put her to bed, and far too old for such exertion, climbed the immense bare stairway with trays for the invalid. Gerta told her stories, sat by the bedside, excited with the drama, with something to do, and with Nordic bravery, plunged majestically into the soiled linen. And worst of all, the nurse told hundreds of stories of ladies and their lovers, treating Jutta all the time as if she were a girl, and worse, as if she were a child. On the final rainy day, when the child could hardly walk, Gerta insisted upon dressing her meticulously and heavily, and tied, grunting, one of the mother's huge old bonnets on her head to shield her, unhappily, from the storm. It was Gerta's care, the coughing attachment and unforgiveable pity, that made the nation's born leader forlorn in the nunnery. How the old fool petted and fawned even before the sisters, who, though not so outwardly comforting, were more, finally, difficult and grasping, feeding on their wards.

The stately steps grew closer; confessions mumbled nearer at hand.

Standing together like obedient black birds at the bottom of the stairway, their heads bent in silent unmeditating respect, the sisters waited until Superior disappeared upwards and out of sight, painfully slow and belligerently in communion. Never, never could she whip these girls into shape, she deplored the ragamuffins, the misplaced childish females. She did not like girls. Superior caught her breath, drew herself up, and made headway through the common lot of problems and despairs, passing unscathed from cell to cell.

The world was growing dimmer for Jutta, the crisis was at hand, her hold on her knees was precarious and sharp. Whether or not she was responsible, she had her weakness, physical and perhaps beyond control, and it made her guilty of disease while the calcium continued to dribble away from the cold, well-bred bones. And despite her praiseworthy nature, her determination, she did fear Superior. Behind all her plotted good intentions, behind her adoration of the East and worship of people in the abstract, the fear always remained, fear of mother, fear of being nursed, fear of Superior. The light was flowing out of the *bunker,* there was nothing more to do except wait for the final unadmitted illusion to disappear, nothing to think of, no one to dislike, no one she needed to love. The little stone-like bumps were hard and rough under her fingers, the hair was straight into her eyes.

"I didn't really want to do it, Superior," the voices were drawing closer with short unpleasant sobs, "I never really wanted to, it was all a mistake, I'm sorry, truly sorry, sorry," and Jutta heard them falling in terror into the slovenly captivity of forgiveness, heard the voices folding into submission. Superior would cross each name, that night, off from the human list. What was it? Yes, she scorned the heroes on *die Heldenstrasse,* they were forgiven, blessed and posed. She would not put on her Sunday shoes to walk that street. But she could not see Superior, she could not, and surely the grey waters of hell would drown her for that treachery, that fear.

The shadows were cold, her hands were unfeeling with numbness. The *Oberleutnant,* warm and restless, tossed off the covers, thought of silken hair and fiery eyes.

Suddenly the light vanished, faster than the moon could be covered with clouds, and the dark angel stood in the doorway cutting off the candlelight from the outside world. The waters opened at the feet of the girl, Superior opened her warm heart, ready to receive the remnants of another mortal. The throat tightened, pulled, and at that moment she heard the General calling, calling from the great room of feasting, "Where is the railroad station, the railroad station?" and he was laughing.

"Child," the woman stayed in the doorway, half in the hall, half inside, "are you ready to open your heart to the Heavenly Father? Are you ready to be insured of safe flight from the pit of everlasting day and weariness? Now is the time to atone." Superior's voice was loud, was always the same whether she was

113

talking to the well or ill, was always clear and harsh. "Now is the time to abandon the wicked man of your soul, now you may come to my arms." She remained rigidly blocking the light. "Child, have you prepared your confession?"

Surely if she lived she would end up a civil official after all, entrusted and forced to take down, patiently, Superior's documents of condemnation. She felt a small, cold throbbing under her arm.

"No." She did not think, but answered dumbly, out of the deathbed. "No. I have nothing to confess, absolutely nothing, nothing." She was talking back to Gerta, telling her brothers to leave her alone, for she was cold and tired. "Nothing to say to you, Superior," and relaxing her grasp, she slipped from the cot, a rude, black, invalidated heap.

The *Oberleutnant,* disturbed by the voices, threw on his trousers and trudged angrily upstairs. This sort of thing had to stop.

Ernie was so small now, propped helplessly in bed, fever and chill making his face now comical, now cruel and saintlike. He was a puppet with two masks and it was up to Stella, weary, to change them as he bid. He had become as bothersome and old as all unhealthy people, but he loved, in the agonizing undramatic last moments of his life, to swallow the thick medicine and make bitter faces. Stella heard from the sentry, who was still posted at the door of the General's empty estate, that the illness was spreading all through the city. He told her rumors of deaths, widespread prostitution, and of imminent victory. "At least," she thought to herself, "dear Ernst is not the only one." The valises were still unpacked and lay crookedly, uncertainly, at the foot of his bed. "He looks," thought Stella, "as if he had a toothache," and indeed the patient's cheeks were swollen and inflamed at the sides of his thin white face. His coat collar was turned up about his throat, it was better to put him straight to bed, even fully dressed. Everywhere Stella moved, he still called, and though his face was turned away, the voice in the depths of his chest, she felt him holding on to her with his last breath of grace. She hadn't even time to wash, the windows were still boarded up, the furniture, except the pile he lay upon, was still in the basement. For the first time since her love on the mountain, she began to realize that he was a fencer in the clouds, stuck through, finally, with a microscopic flu. The room was dark and close as sickrooms are, but the evening chill and ageless year-round dampness made it more like an underground aid station. Holding her breath she leaned over the averted face, pulled it to position, pushed the sugar-grimed spoon between the lips, and straightened with a long sigh.

Stella didn't know what she would do with him when he died. All at once the problem was overwhelming, his remains would hang around for weeks. The idea of disposal seemed so remote and impossible. Surely the man who took care of such things would be long out of business, where could she turn? If only the body would fly away with the soul, but, no, it would linger on, linger on here in this very room. "He doesn't look at all," she thought, "like the man I married in the garden." Where is the railroad station? She helped him through each physical minute, becoming more impatient as he coughed and turned. Suddenly it struck her that this was not old Herman's son, and now she was nursing a stranger, not even a ward of the State. "Dear Ernst," she thought, "you look just like Father."

Every time he opened his eyes, he saw her there, warm, beautiful, efficient. The very breath of the flowers on her shoulder brought new life. When she sat on the bed, one soft dark knee upon the other, one thin elbow pushing gently against her bosom, holding the lovely head, all lofty desire was his, he was in the presence of the white lady of the other world. Ah, to die no longer with the fire but with the dove. The first stages of death took energy, the last mere confidence. The closer she bent with the spoon in her hand, the warmer he felt, the farther he flew.

"Stella?"

"Yes, Ernst?"

"Isn't it time for the black pills?"

Immediately she brought the bottle.

"Herman, stay away," he thought. "The old man must not come back, the wonderful peace of being waited on must not be broken. The corrupter's prime agent should not be allowed out of the war, but should stay forever and ever in some black hole away from the gracious light of Heaven. The maiden voyage of the star, all hands accounted for, safely arrived into the sky. At last to be able to do something alone, without old Snow there to beat the other fellow's back." The dreams arose more vividly, he forgot the star. "Those were fearful times with the old man filled with wrath. Oh, no, that demon could not possibly come back to plague my end, to expect to be welcomed home at such a precarious, serious time." Ernst channeled himself once more into the soft light, the medicine smelled as sweet as the valor-petals, without the demon's horned masterful voice intruding.

"He flicked his eyes open and shut once," Stella later told the guard.

"Stella." He called again, "Stella, in the carpetbag, he's there, somewhere near the bottom, get him, please."

She rummaged through the flabby thing, like a peddler's sack, and there, beneath the newspapers and photographs, sure enough, under the soiled shirt, near the bottom on a pair of black shoes, it lay, wrapped in old Christmas tissue.

"Here." He patted the pillow near his cheek, "Here," he said in bliss.

She put the carving of Christ, almost as large as his head, on the pillow. She waited as if for something to happen. How peculiar, the wooden man and fleshless God, they kept good company. Then she remembered: on the mountain she too lay by Christ, and it was a mistake!

Suddenly he coughed and the little statue rolled over, its arms and legs thrown wide in fear.

"Here," she said, "now drink this, drink it." For a moment it looked as if he would recover. Then, no, no, he smiled again and all was lost. Stella crossed her soft dark knees.

The guard did not bother to open the door for Gerta and Herr Snow, but whistled and wondered at the old woman's return, while the soldier and his girl pushed alone into the darkness of the wide downstairs hall. For a moment, Gerta stood uncertainly in the middle of the vacant foyer, listening for the sounds of the dead, with Herman leaning, drugged, on her arm. She could hear the guard, the last guard, behind her shuffling about on the other side of the door. Herman breathed heavily in the darkness, his weight sagged, she could see nothing. Then she heard them, those dead two, master and mistress, and far overhead she saw a line of light and heard the tinkle of glass, ghosts in their cups.

She wanted to shut the soldier, shirt off, shoes off, into her room with all night, every night for no telling how long, before her. But she began to lead him toward the light. Mistake, mistake to bring such a tender man, so close to popping, within the realm of unwanted, unexpected guests—to let the steam off the wrong end, the end of white, flat apprehension. And she too, by walking up the stairs, was holding off. As they neared the top, he tripped once, twice, and Gerta began to cross the line from love to nurse, from grand-sharer to assistant.

It was Fraulein Stella's room. They waited before the door.

The trains were still arriving. Under cover of darkness, small and squat, they emptied themselves of soldiers home on leave. In the dark the girls milling on the platform could not tell whether the trains were full of passengers, perhaps men, or empty. Signals crossed, whistles argued out of the stops of tangled rail, "Train from 31, train from 9, let me pass, I'm carrying wounded." "Wait, you'll have to wait, 31, there are dogs in front."

Gerta could hear the whistles far out in the night. They were long and old-fashioned and far away.

"Do you hear the dogs?" Ernst spoke, hands picking at the covers.

"Of course, dear husband."

He could hear them barking among the boat whistles in the middle of the night.

Stella mixed the potions and wondered about the hour, what could she do when the hour stopped? All about her the phials, the wads of cotton, the handbook of medical instruction, were out of reach, too slow. There was nothing she could do against it, she lost her place in the handbook. All the soft embrace of the mountain was gone, all the humor of his saber wounds was healed; he was stitched and shrouded in that impertinent, unthinking smile. He grew thinner, and staring her full in the face with his three fingers twitching helplessly on the cover, he gagged.

They heard the scratching at the door and at first they thought it was the wind, only the comforting night air.

"Now, what's she doing here," thought Gerta as she stepped into the patient's room with her lover behind.

The red-bearded devil leaned across the bed, staring at the man with a toothache. Herman looked from his son to Stella, the lovely girl, from the colored bottles to the boarded window, and back to the majestic bed.

"He's not sick!" and the devil roared with laughter, his desire for Gerta flickering out in spasms of recognition of his foe, the bedded influenza.

He had horns. Terrible, agonizing, deformed short stubs protruding from the wrinkled crown, and the pipes he held in his fiery hands were the pipes of sin. All of the calm of Heaven evaporated and at the last moment, not knowing what it was all about, Ernst recognized Old Snow. And in that moment of defense, of hating the devilish return of boisterous heroic Herman, Ernst died without even realizing the long-awaited event; in that last view of smallness, that last appearance of the intruder, Ernst, with his mouth twisted into dislike, died, and was reprieved from saintliness. The old man still laughed, "Feigning, he's only feigning!" Stella was irritated with his ignorance, at least this father could rise to the dignity of the occasion by admitting the fact of death. But no, he chuckled and looked stupid.

Herman paid for his mirth, for it had stolen his son and his stamina. He slept uncomfortably with Gerta in the room which she felt was much too small for the rest of the night.

The guard, Stella found, managed in the morning to fulfill her final obligation to the dead. The disbelief and anger were still on the fencer's face as he was carried from the house, saved by the grace of his own ill-luck and ill-will.

Jutta awoke with the vision of spectacles and hood still in the abbey room and out of the weak unending dream, she heard the tinkle of the goodnight bell, while the pain in her arms and legs was numbed by her victory; for Superior was gone.

"Jutta, Jutta, go to bed," but she discounted that voice. The last authority was gone. Superior, rebuffed, sat at her desk down the hall, unable to write, so angry, the cowl that covered her fierce shaved head tossed aside on a chair. The waiting woman stared in concern at the nun turned monk.

Jutta tried to move, but could not, and stayed for a moment, her face turned to the floor, rising from the squeamish pit of the too-easy psalm and too-easy dying bone. She opened her eyes. "There are enemies even within our own State," she remembered and wondered why the *Oberleutnant* didn't stop Superior, and she was glad to know, being allowed to wake once more, that life was not miraculous but clear, not right but undeniable. How narrow and small was the suffocating Superior with part of each day spent bartering with the miraculous medal salesman. Jutta felt, being once more back in the cell where Gerta put her, uncomfortably sick and very tired. She would try to reach the cot.

The nunnery, high and safe within the meek heart, far from the blockade at sea, rested confident and chaste in the middle of the night, spreading its asylum walls outwards over a few bare feet of uninhabited dry earth. Safe, within the Allied querulous dragnet, because a taste of faith was all the inmates knew, because over the years, the hearts grew large and the stomachs naturally small, safe, with the cyclical event of mother, girl, and vanity thrown out. The old white barn rocked gently in the cloudy night. The moss had grown thin, turned brown, and died on the mud walls, water no longer trickled and grew thick in the well, the sand could hardly lift itself through the halls at night on the wind's back, but still in the morning and evening, bells faithfully chimed out the remote and tedious day. "Father, save me," thinking of the girls, "from these merciless infidels," said Superior, and leaning forward, she shrouded herself in darkness and sat for a long while with her pains and troubles by the window.

An oyster shell on the beach far away was shrouded in oil, coming in off the treacherous tide. The dogs barked.

"Perhaps I should call a doctor," thought the *Oberleutnant* bending over the sick girl, but at that moment she stirred, and besides, he remembered, the old horse that used to be in the stables and could have made the journey to the surgeon's house, was dead.

Jutta could not reach the cot, but slowly her anger and childish pain brought her back from the fleece-lined pit, and at that moment, she heard the bell in the tower ring three, heard Superior, who had rung it, padding back, feelings still hurt, to sit by the window. With a sudden lucky gesture, Jutta turned her head upwards, and in the dim light stared at the uncovered masculine chest of the *Oberleutnant* as he bent down, watching her on the floor.

Then, that night, she passed the crisis, and breath by breath, though scrutinized and unloved, she assumed more of life, still alone, more silent, colder than ever.

A few months after the death of Ernst, Stella gave birth to her fragile son, and while she was still on the bearing bed, Gerta and Herman took the child from her, carried it and kept it, down in the first-floor dark pleasure room where they had failed together that first night. Food became more scarce, and Stella never forgave the old woman for the stolen son. Hearing the dogs howling around the station at the port of entry to the grave, she thought, once more, of singing. The Christ carving had disappeared.

PART THREE—1945

TONIGHT

All during the day the villagers had been burning out the pits of excrement, burning the fresh trenches of latrines where wads of wet newspapers were scattered, burning the dark round holes in the back stone huts where moisture traveled upwards and stained the privy seats, where pools of water became foul with waste that was as ugly as the aged squatter. These earthen pots were still breathing off their odor of burned flesh and hair and biddy, and this strange odor of gas and black cheese was wafted across the roads, over the fields, and collected on the damp leaves and in the bare night fog along the embankment of the *Autobahn*. This smell not only rested over the mud, but moved, and with every small breath of air, the gas of mustard, soft goat pellets and human liquid became more intimate, more strong and visible in reddening piles. One's own odor could always be sifted out and recognized, a disturbingly fresh stream in the turning ash, a personal mark that could be sniffed and known after midnight, sometimes as if the tongue were poking in the incinerator and the warm air curling about the hewn seat.

The three of us waited by the side of the road, stockingless feet burning and itching in our unlaced shoes, plucking at nostrils, listening to a wasted mongrel paw the leaves, hearing an occasional tile slide from a roof and fall to the mud with the swishing of a tail. The flats turned away before us, un-peopled, dark, an occasional shell-case filling with seepage, the fingers of a lost glove curling with dew. Behind us the ghosts left the stalled tank and filed downward toward the canal.

"He's late," said Fegelein.

"Yes."

"No sleep for us then."

"Wait, have patience," I answered.

We crowded invisibly together with the road high overhead that extended far beyond this edge of town, and there were no precision transits or plumb lines to point the kilometers of travel or show the curve on the map where the blank spot of this town would be. We never ventured away, though we still wore the grey shirts and had signed our way to the out-side world.

"It's a good machine he's riding," said Fegelein.

"Don't worry. I won't shoot at it."

"Good."

"Remember, no talking. Stintz would be sure to say something when the next rider comes through in a month looking for this one." I constantly had to give commands.

"In a month we'll be ready."

"Yes."

"And the motorbike will be useful."

"Yes." I had to humor them.

In every town there are a few who, though they don't remember how it came about, or how they returned, or when they went away, or what the enemy expects, gather together in the night to rise again, despite the obstacle of their own people or the swarming invader. Behind us the town grew smaller; the sleepers were cold and numberless.

"No one will see?"

"No," I answered.

"I don't want to go forward tonight; you mustn't make me . . ."

"Stop that. You know there isn't any forward."

"I'm sorry."

The cold night air quickened my hunger, and I put the thought out of mind, concentrated on the hunched man in goggles and helmet. Once the old horse clattered by above our ears and then moved off as if he smelled nothing, neither fresh grass nor humans nearby.

Jutta's child watched in the window, her sharp eyes darting this way and that among the shadows, hands folded in her lap, knees drawn together, small and wide awake as children who follow the night very long after the usual time to sleep, quickened and tense with the unexpected hours, wretched small keepers. But she did not see her brother, the fairy, nor any forms crawling along the street among the ends of broken pipe. She watched for a light, a swinging lantern, or any recognizable animal or man in the bare branches and felt that she must wait and watch, for she knew that all were not asleep. She waited for Jutta as a child would, and saying nothing she called her mother home. What was the hour? No one could know because there were no clocks. She knew the time by intuition, this dark time, as a thing that ended only with sleep. She knew that one could never see the morning come, and only by turning away, by hiding, would the night leave. For a long while it had been quiet below, from the time Herr Stintz stopped playing his horn until now, and by a few unnatural sounds, the rustling of cloth, the dropping of a shoe, she knew

127

he was no longer asleep. He was fetching his stick. Jutta didn't like him either, because he could commit no crime nor act strongly, but could only bring harm. The child heard the splash of water and then waited, hearing him walk the length of his cage and unlock the door.

The fairy, out of sight, was running for his life.

She was afraid to look at him and barely made a gesture as if to touch the window, thinking to strike up a light.

"It's very late for a little girl to be out of bed, away from the covers, the nice warm quilt."

"I'm waiting for my brother."

"But you should sleep, because the moon doesn't like little girls to look into his bed. The moon sleeps in the world, a very strong man, and God has given him no covers."

"He's not sleeping tonight."

Mr. Stintz could only bring harm; she knew he carried the stick, but knew that little girls were safe because they were the ones who waited and never moved. If she moved, the paw would break off her wing and catch her by the leg.

"Oh," she said, "there's my mother."

"Why don't you," he said, "why don't we look for the moon quickly?"

She heard the door shut gently. Death is in the breaking of a lock, a cut in the skin, it comes with a cough and leaves before the plaster is dry on the chest. Stintz drove the boys in the rain and made the girls repeat and repeat their lessons in the old schoolroom, and no one spoke to him in the streets. "Madame Snow told me to die . . ." Then she saw something more wonderful than mother, something unknown but unmistakable. A light flashed in the distance, and as she watched, it drew closer, a thin quavering beam that seemed to be searching its way out of the darkness. This was what she had waited for and now she no longer watched for her brother but crept off under the covers. It was as if she had just visited the empty apartment on the second floor.

"Good night," she heard her mother say.

The three of us leaning against the clay bank were all that remained of the shadows of sentries, were primal, unordered, unposted sentries, lounging against the earth without password, rifles or relief. The sharp foreign voice had disappeared from the dark road and unlighted doorway, the rolls of wire, the angry tones, the organized guards were gone. Though unmistakable signs remained, a trampled package of woodbines, a tossed-off canteen, a piece of white webbing, these scraps still littered the floors of sheds or hung in the room corners where white women lay. The keepers, who had asked for papers, swore only with one word, lighted the night with red, and confiscated bicycles, and had moved on to the hunting ground of rodents. And we, the three shadows who remained, gaunt for the great land, dependent on the enemy's tin cans to squat in, waiting in our black unbuttoned coats and peaked caps, were sentries of the civilians, unemployed during the day, plotting for the greatest good by night.

The American on the motorcycle knew no more of the country that his eagle-colonels scourged, than did his free-eyed sergeants, roving in their green work clothes. He traveled along hypothetical lines of communication that chased miles beyond the end of the war and he had beer at each stopover. Desperation was not for this plains-rider, bouncing over once endless roads with his sack filled with unintelligible military scrawl, columns of figures, personal resentments, not for this oblivious traveler whose only communication was silence to the dark countrymen and "hi-ya, Mac" to his listless fellows. From the littered fields and overhanging branches, from the town library charred and unpurged, from the punctured rubber rafts plugging the canal, to the hanging mouths, to the enemy colors, to the unexploded traps, to the drunk official and black pox, it was an unrecognized, unadmitted, unnamed desperation that persisted beyond the tied prostitute and enemy news, beyond the cadaverous houses and American outposts, to give strength to us, the hovering sentries, to bring words to the lolling historians. Poison their camps, if only in a quip or solitary act.

I thought of it during each day in the newspaper office and thought of it against the mud-bank; life is not the remarkable, the precious, or necessary thing we think it is. The naked dark pawing of that eternal old horse who lingered on through no fault of his own, bereaved and unquiet in the night, told me that. And with the hoarded, secret sailor's black rum running through my mind, heaped about by past years' correspondence, dead letters, by fragments of broken type, I knew that the tenant was the law. For the final judgment the tenant must build the house and keep it from sliding into the pool, keep it from the Jew's claw or the idealist's pillaging.

You can ask no man to give up his civilization, which is his nation. The old must go, stagger over the failing drawbridge, fall down before the last coat of arms. I thought Madame Snow too old to understand, I thought she should wither away and die, with her long, false, flaxen hair, because I thought she would run rattle-tattle through the night for preservation. Here I was wrong, since she was the very hangman, the eater, the greatest leader of us all. Death is as unimportant as life; but the struggle, the piling of bricks, the desperate attempts of the tenant; that is the man of youth, the old woman of calm, the nation of certainty.

I brushed the hair away from my ears, relaxed against the earthen wall, smelled the flowering manure.

"Soon?" Even old Stumpfegel was impatient.

"Certainly. Have patience."

The child was not yet asleep, the drains were running foul to the basement, the Mayor dreamed, heaping one on another all the atrocities his old heart could dig up, so that they rolled in a paroxysm in his throat. The windows were shut, but he could not guard against the tottering dreams—for honoring the dead he must die. An attempt to stir himself with his own hand, since his wife was long gone, was, like the ventures of foraging children, like their touch to the self, a breath of suicide. Long after he was disturbed by the noise under the window, the dream returned and forced its way, lifelike, before his eyes as if he were awake. Dream after dream the voices and horses were the same, though they wore many figures, the Priest mixed up with the Officer, his own dead wife firing the rifle, a peculiar child pronouncing verdict as the Judge, the onlooking crowd all dressed as the condemned man. But the voices were distinct, and waking he would forget that they had calmly passed sentence, enemies and friends—guilty in the eyes of his own State.

He had betrayed the country only through his conscience . . .

Madame Snow held Balamir's hand.

The child could not sleep and listened to the mother's breathing.

Dancers wearied and each time the record stopped, the silence made them anxious.

The wind struggled and sighed and could go no farther than the edge of the canal.

A cow with its eyes shut clawed at the empty board walls of a barn with teeth like a hare but found no straw.

The boy had gotten himself lost in underworld tunnels, caught between hanging floors and rolls of wire, and he caught his pants on a bent thick nail.

The Duke followed closely in his step, cane raised sharply in the darkness, feeling his way carefully into the blind hole, and it began to rain. The tall man followed the boy through the gaping plaster wall and found himself in the theater. Madame Snow's one-legged son and noiseless wife were somewhere overhead near the projection room. The boy traveled in circles among the thousands of molding seats while rain trickled down the sloping floor and a field telephone covered with dust looked like an enormous trap on a chain. The theater grew darker. Carefully the Duke followed the shadows, slid like an elder actor to the ticket-seller's booth and doffing his hat stepped through the door and waited, surrounded with black glass, rolls of wet tickets, a red handkerchief. A rotted playbill masked his face. He saw something walk across the stage in false breasts and tights, heard the boy drawing fitfully near.

". . . It is you who will die," said the Priest to the Mayor. That had been the day when the motorcycle rider and the rest of the Allies had first passed through *Spitzen-on-the-Dein*. The convoy crept up the long bright highway through the snow, through the handful of silent watchers, down the main street like a centipede with the motorcycle first, followed by the jeep, ending with proud band of four riflemen. An American colonel and two corporals rode in the jeep, an automatic rifle propped in the back seat, their canteens filled with rum, and the dispatch-rider in the lead wobbled from side to side and waved the children off, flurries of snow shooting up behind him.

"So this is Germany," said the Colonel, and leaning out from behind the cold wheel he blew his whistle and the convoy stopped. Before the eyes of the crowd he got out and fastened a slender wire-cutter to the smoking radiator, then with a final quick word to the motorcycle man they made their way to the center of town, pulling on their mufflers, eyes frozen ahead. On the floor of the jeep beneath the jutting rifle, they carried their black robes and a few sealed envelopes. The foot-soldiers alternately ran and walked to keep warm.

By the middle of the afternoon they had stripped Madame Snow's apartment and established a headquarters, of three maps, a table and chair, temporary seat of American representation in the evil zone. The jeep was under a tarpaulin in the rear garden in the shed, the four troops billeted in the hall, and the dispatch rider was standing guard over his still warm machine. Through the uncurtained window, glancing for a moment from the red envelopes, the Colonel saw the sky darken for snow, and worried, he peered at his highly secret route through the nation, studied the undecipherable diagram and code. Satisfied, he signaled the corporal who quickly brought forth the three robes. The Colonel, short, heavyset, graduate of a technical institute, a brilliant engineer, thought in dotted parabolas, considered in fine red lines, and while lonely, overworked, and short in the knees, directed the spreading occupation. Except for the silver eagle sewn above the pocket of his black robe, he might have been the foreman of a jury pointed out to speak before the supreme law. Once more he carefully read the letter of instruction, tapped his pen on the bare wood, then dropped the paper into the heater in the corner, an open can of flaming petrol. The Mayor, Herr Stintz and myself stood in a corner, as there was no anteroom, watching these preparations, while out in the cold alone, walking up and down, waited Miller, the prisoner, thinking of the sweet children and his fair wife.

The robed men muttered together at the far end of the room behind the table, and we three, the witnesses, waited while a thin soot from the burning can settled over the floor, the walls, collected on the Colonel's two musette bags and on the neat small row of cracking army boots. The maps, freshly tacked to the wall, grew darker and the chill in the air grew worse with the promise of snow, soot speckled the grease on the Colonel's mess tins tied to the bedroll. Once one of the corporals turned, "No talking there," and we did not understand, for only the Colonel spoke German. Then, after a short silence, the Colonel seemed to remember. "My God, Corporal, get my pistol—and you might bring my pipe." The young man, holding the black hem above his boots, scowled once at us, the witnesses, and searched in one of the small dirty bags. Then a pause while they fumbled under his gown to arm him and he lit the pipe, his black cassock skirt and tough hands stiff with cold. The motorcycle rider's white helmet moved back and forth across the window, scattered flakes of snow dropped on his jacket.

"Mayor," the corporal called, and the frightened old man stepped into the dock, tensed for a dangerous question.

The Colonel took his place and spoke:

"How old are you?"

"Eh, what's that?"

"Your age, age."

"I'm sixty-one." His paper collar wilted, the official sash sagged on his waist, and he was afraid.

"Where were you born?"

"Right here, here in this very place."

"I understand you keep some sort of civil records?"

"I did, quite true, very fine writing. But they're gone, burned up, shells hit my house, zip, zip, and in the fallen glass the flames spread, so my papers are all gone."

"Well, I want to know something about," the Colonel looked at his notes, "a man named Miller."

"I've known him for years, his wife, children."

"Now, is it true he was a pastor?"

"Pastor? Ah, yes, pastor."

"But now he no longer is?"

"No longer? Well, not actively, the war, I don't think there were many people to listen . . ."

"Did he *want* to stop being a pastor?"

"Well, there was a good deal of trouble in this town, we suffered . . ."

I called from the corner, "He *is* a pastor."

"Silence, keep quiet, there."

Then Herr Stintz came forward, a primer under his arm, smiling, and he edged himself in front of the Mayor.

"If you'll permit me," he said.

"Well, what is it?"

Stintz stepped closer, glasses pinching over his nose. "Herr Colonel, I think perhaps you should take into account that there was, you know, a new gospel, the war made a change in what a man might want to preach to the dumb people—other ears heard, the new gospel was a very strong thing, even his wife could do nothing with Miller."

The Colonel looked for a long moment at the Mayor.

"Is this true? Was there a change in Miller?"

"Well, everyone, the war was a hard thing but," the old man found himself staring at the eagle on the Colonel's chest, and it seemed to glow with a phosphorescent sheen, "but I'm alone, I don't know him that well, he was away . . ." The eagle grew bright and the old man wiped his chin, tried to fasten the sash tighter, "but I think, maybe, he did change . . ."

"He did not," I said.

"He's a tough one," whispered the officer to the corporal, pointing at me, and the judges retired. The snow fell harder, the rider covered his bike with a gunnysack. "I think," said the Colonel, "that the case is closed, but we better be just, it will be excellent to impress them with our thoroughness." So for the rest of the afternoon, while the snow became thick and we waited in the corner, while one of the corporals took notes and the can ran out of fuel, a long line of civilians was formed and one by one each citizen of the town passed into the dark room, was questioned, and was returned to the raw cold evening. At last the entire population had come and gone, steel slats had been driven across the cellar window where Miller waited, and the Colonel undid his bedroll and lay down in the deep rich fur to sleep out the night. Long afterwards the Mayor blamed everything on the shining eagle, "It had frightful curled claws and a sharp hooked nose with red terrifying eyes. That's what it did to me."

The Colonel shook himself awake before dawn, five o'clock by his wrist watch accurate as a micrometer, and in only his grey underwear donned a long sheepskin field coat and stumbled into the day's work. Moving about in the dark hallway where his riflemen lay, he left a bright blank cartridge by each man and emptied each weapon of its live ammunition, inspecting each oiled chamber and silver whirling bore. Back in the long bare living room he filled the petrol tin and, hunched in the great curling coat, made himself a pot of black coffee, warming, the while, his hands over the small flame. The Mayor, Stintz and I slept together in the corner, the corporals were buried deep in their cots, and in the basement, trapped amid the piles of debris, Miller waited to see the morning through the narrow slats. The Colonel busied himself with a worn grammar, put his mess kit aside to be cleaned, and let his men sleep for another hour. Finally, ten minutes before six, he dug into his gear and pulled forth his best garrison cap, polished the badge with a rag, left it ready for the important hour and then padded out of doors. His were the first prints through the snow in the back yard; he was the first to break the air still heavy as with waiting flakes. The canal smelled strongly of vermin and slapping rubber, a broken rake handle and emery wheel jutted up through the damp snow, no smoke came from the chimneys on the other bank. Plough handles, shafts of wood, caked earthenware, the jaws of a wooden vice, old scraps of leather filled the slanting shed where the jeep was garaged under the tarpaulin, and a spot of thick green oil spread over the dirt floor. Two planks, nailed along one thin wall that was once a work bench, were bare—for all pieces of metal, tools, iron wheels had been melted down for shells— bare except for a pair of faded pink pants left on one end, shriveled to the size of a fist. The door swung shut behind the Colonel, he rummaged about the shed, thought of the Fraulein who owned the pants, caught with long braids and bright smile, then he reached into the jeep and pulled out another rifle, bright and clean. The odor of chickens, old herbs, mold, mixed with the oil, and he heard the slapping of low water in the canal, trickling over layers and shreds of thin ice. He checked the tires, looked once more about the shed, then walked back to his headquarters across the unkempt white garden.

By six o'clock he had waked the men, decided that the roads were passable and had loaded the new rifle with a live cartridge.

"Here now, Leevey," he called out the window to the still-walking dispatch rider, "you handle the prisoner this morning." Then, while the three of us sat up and blinked, the Colonel shaved, peering into a mechanical mirror that had crooked collapsible legs. After he was dressed, one of the corporals brushed his uniform, helped him bundle back into the heavy coat, and handed him the cap with the bright badge.

By six-thirty the whole town had been raised and stood crammed together in the garden and the motorcycle rider fastened the red cloth about Miller's eyes while, he, the prisoner, stood rigidly on the edge of the canal. The Colonel hurried out, followed by the Mayor, Stintz, and me, and his troop, hurried to see that Miller was placed correctly, checked the time. Though the sky was heavy, he was sure it would not snow, and if they got an early start should be able to cover two hundred miles at least. "Come," he said turning to me, "I need another rifleman. You just take this gun and fall in line with my men." He handed me the new weapon, the fifth, well greased, light, loaded, then arranged our squad in good order. "Mayor," he called, "Mayor, come here." The old man trembled and came forward, his nose grey with the cold, his chest hollow. The Colonel reached into a woollen pocket and brought forth a large white handkerchief, thrust it upon the shivering leader. "Now you hold this over your head, and when you see me nod, drop it." All right, Leevey," called the Colonel, "come away from the prisoner." The water slid by in the canal. Stintz watched carefully, eager for justice, the Census-Taker, drunk, leaned on Madame Snow's arm and held Jutta's hand, watched the white cloth drooping in the dull morning.

"Leevey," said the Colonel when they were abreast, speaking in a lowered voice, "you might see about loading the jeep, we have a long way to go today."

The crowd grew restless, a thin sickly pink began to stain the clouds, the four men and myself raised our short barrels while the two bow ends of the Pastor's red bandanna flapped in a light breeze.

139

His upraised arm began to pain, and the Mayor felt his legs knocking together, backwards and forwards, and he thought he would perish with the cold. Then he caught the glance from the man with the big eagle on his cap and his fingers opened. "It is you who will die," called the Pastor, and the Mayor shut his eyes.

The noise of the rifles sounded small and muffled, padded in the heavy air, and his fingers still felt as if they held the cloth. Miller fell back, dropped through the film of ice and floated jerkily down over the shoals, catching against rocks, dragging over pieces of wood, bumping the flabby rafts, the red cloth flashing for a moment.

"You're a good shot," the Colonel said to me, "that's the gun that did it." The Census-Taker had to be carried back to the house.

A half-hour later the convoy rolled out onto the highway, jeep coughing, the Colonel carefully driving, leaving behind the several posters and proclamations that the motorcycle-rider had pasted up to the peeling walls: "The Government of the United States . . ." For the most part, they were unreadable.

The Mayor thought they were watching him. The sheets were soiled, the Pastor, holding the book, tapped at the shutters, the bird picked at his toes and he took sick because they talked under his window and his conscience was soft, soft as the pink pants . . .

"My God, he's not coming at all!" said Fegelein.

"Don't be a fool, it's almost time." Sometimes I had to be harsh.

"You don't think he'll see the log and stop?"

"Of course not."

I myself began to wich that the *Schmutz* on the little motorcycle would hurry up, morning would soon come and the newspaper office would be waiting, the old women with their bright eyes would be out watching in the streets, the dumb children would be snooping. The land is important, not the *Geist;* the bronx-mongolians, the fat men, the orators, must be struck down. The three of us, the sentries, drew closer together in the low fog.

Herr Stintz, alone in the dark, stood by the open window and listened, looked up at the starless sky, pointed his snout towards the apartment above, straining his muzzle. He, feeling the small girl so close, hearing her breath, felt some of her apprehension, and wide awake did not think of the cold bare walls behind him, or of the pieces of cracked furniture, but concentrated on the heavens, and spied, waiting to see what would happen. And thinking how small and white she was, he tried to divine her secret, thrust his head farther out of the casement, a head that was white, high and narrow, that leaned around corners to hear, and crinkled about the pale eyes with spying. Stintz was hostile to the cold April night air, peered back and forth across the lowering sky, held the birch stick under his arm. He heard Jutta's footsteps overhead as she readied for sleep and pretended to himself that the mother would take the child into her own bed. The nighty was soft and covered with tender prints and only came to the thin knees, the little neckline was flat against the chest.

Madame Snow, erect, frail, wrapped a quilt about Balamir's shoulders where he kneeled on the floor, and by the light of the candle studied the poor creature's face. She found herself listening for footsteps of the second floor roomer, for she knew that the apartment was empty and dark.

The Mayor awoke, wept momentarily, and reached under the bed for a round receptacle. He wanted to know if morning was close but was afraid to open the shutter.

The theater was vast, the audience dead ratters, forgotten bits of paper left on the seats, wet, loose, covered with growth. The drizzle had ceased and a slight wind swept down the aisles, stirring fragments of celluloid, springs, and old playbills. The Duke waited.

"Would you like to buy a ticket?" And his voice still echoing and booming from the cage to the proscenium in unfamiliar strained tones as he stepped from behind the glass and faced the crouched boy.

With winter almost gone, the coagulated underground pipes began to loosen and a thin dark stream of drained seepage flowed, connected every low basement, and trickled about, encircled all the dog-used walls.

Then Herr Stintz heard a voice, small and calm, soft under the covers, "Mother, I saw a light!" And quickly the thin snapping man glanced down over the village, watched the trees, strained his ears upwards, but could hear nothing except a peculiar puttering. Then he saw it, feeble as a flashlight, weak as an old woman's lantern used behind the house, swaying blindly as a bat's eye, gone out behind a sagging barn, free again over the bushes, lost behind a high gate, and then at last it was clear and unbroken, and Stintz, greedy, pop-mouthed, watched it circle slowly along the great curve of, he realized, the *Autobahn*.

At the same time we three heard the sound of the isolated engine as the bastard on the motor approached.

"I'll get him in the behind—*behind*," I whispered.

The light flared once and went out.

LEADER

A hundred miles from *Spitzen-on-the-Dein* in the early morning of the day when the killing occurred, the intended victim, Leevey, lay wearied and injured beside a laughing slut who was covered with invisible red clap. All through the darkness they had struggled, baring each other with the point of a knee, angry and calling each other *schmuck,* and she had struck his face so that the eyes bled. She raised her white legs above the sheets, then grimaced and threw him off, jabbing with her fists as he fell against the wall. Over and over she said, "My house, you come to *my* house," but Leevey was afraid that if he left the safety of his room she would shellac him, cut with the scissors, and finally leave him dead with a pin through his neck. For he had heard the stories, stories of murder in the empty lot, the special deaths, the vaginae packed with deadly poison. He clung to her, "You stay here," and her sharp wooden sandals sliced at his shins and her unwashed hair fell over his aching shoulder. His white helmet, goggles, and gauntlets lay beside the bunk, his tunic and trousers the girl used as a pillow. "Candy," she said, pinching and poking with her strong fingers. "Go to hell," he whined and the forearm crushed down on his nose and mouth, bruising and dull. Finally, unsuccessful, Leevey tried to sleep, but she scratched and pushed, whistled in his ear, squeezed, cried, jammed with her feet, and just as he dozed would slap with all her strength.

The sun gradually brightened the grey walls, the girl's white laughing eyes never left his face, a quick pinch. The heavy tiredness and pain swept over him and he wished he was back in the delicatessen, his long nose pushed among the cheeses.

When she reached the door she turned, leaned her shoulder against the jamb, thrust out her hip and smiled at the feeble one, also filmed now with red invisible clap, tousled and unprotesting, sick in the bunk:

"Auf Wiedersehen, Amerikaner," she said, *"Amerikaner!"*

Leevey doused his face in the basin, slicked down his black hair. "That's life," he said, "that's life," and as the sun rose clear and cold he slung the Sten-gun on his back, polished his boots, fastened the gauntlets, climbed on his rusty motorcycle, and began the tour of his district.

He traveled ninety miles with his palms shivering on the steerhorn handlebars, the white cold air glazed endlessly ahead, his insides smacking against the broad cowhide saddle. He stopped a few times beside an abandoned farm or mis-turned sign or unburied Allied corpse to take a few notes, laying the machine on its side in the mud, and he sweated over the smeared pad and stubby pencil. He was overseer for a sector of land that was one-third of the nation and he frowned with the responsibility, sped along thinking of the letters he would write home, traveled like a gnome behind a searchlight when the sun finally set and the foreign shadows settled. He saw the bare spire rising less than a mile beyond, and crouching down, spattered with grease, he speeded up, to go past *Spitzen-on-the-Dein* with a roar. The late night and crowded broken road twisted around him, flames shot up from the exhaust.

"Wait a minute, I'll be right up, *Kinder,*" called Herr Stintz to the upper window. He caught one last glimpse of the slim light with its tail of angry short tongues of fire like a comet, and flinging on a thin coat he bolted for the stairs. He made noise, hurried, was neither meek nor ineffectual, for he felt at last he had the right, the obligation, and his tattling could be open, commanding; for he had seen the light, the unexpected journeyman, the foreign arrival, a fire in the night that no one knew about but he, and now he moved without caution, tripping and whispering, to take possession. Again he opened the door to the top floor apartment, hurried through the first room past the unwaking Jutta where her high breast gleamed from under the sheet, past the full basin and into the smaller, cold lair. "Quickly," he said, "we must hurry. It's up to you and me." She made no protest but watched him with sharp appraising eyes, holding her breath. Stintz picked the little girl from the bundle of clothes, wrapped her in a shortened quilt, tied it with string around her waist, fastened the thick stockings on her feet. He knew exactly what he was about as he dressed the child, considered no question, gave no thought to the sleeping mother. Never before had he been so close; he tied the quilt high about her throat, smoothed the hair once quickly with his hand.

"The moon will see," she murmured, as his good eye swept over her.

"No, no, there isn't any moon at all. Come along."

They walked past the woman, hand in hand, into the bitter hallway and he carried her down the stairs, slipped, caught himself, in the hurry. They left the front door ajar and began their walk over the streets smelling of smoke.

The ghosts raised their heads in unison by the canal and sniffed the night air.

I, Zizendorf, my gun drawn, crouching on my knees with my comrades who were tensed like sprinters or swimmers, heard above gusts of wind the approaching light machine. The uprising must be successful, inspired, ruthless.

The Duke carefully reached out his hand and the boy fairy did not move, while the marquee banged to and fro, the projector steamed, and the invisible lost audience stamped booted feet and rummaged in box lunches.

Unconscious, drowned cold in acid, the Census-Taker lay on the third floor, dressed, uncovered, where Jutta had dropped him.

The Mayor, at this hour, groaned, awoke, and found himself pained by a small black-pebble cluster of hemorrhoids, felt it blister upwards over his spine.

The ghosts returned to their cupped hands and sipped the green water, while soft faecal corbans rolled below their faces through the cluttered waves in tribute to Leevey.

Madame Snow thought for a moment that she heard Herr Stintz's voice yelling somewhere up above through the darkest part of the night and drew the robe closer about the kneeling man. Balamir trembled with being awake, frowned and grinned at the old woman, shook as if he was starving on these sleepless hours, tried to speak of the mob of risers, the strength, fear, out in the night, but could not. Stella wondered what they were doing, this anonymous nation, and felt, such an old woman, that she would never sleep again. The candle swayed, her powdered hands fluttered and moved, and then she heard Stintz's sharp footfall and the padding of the girl, and when they left, a breath of air from the front door ajar swept across the floor and stirred the draped figure of her kneeling charge.

Neither could sleep, and somehow the hard yellow eyes of their brethren had told them men were moving, the night was not still. Madame Snow did not find the rooms changed by this darkness or added cold, simply the cups eluded her fingers, slipped more easily, the tea was like black powder and too much escaped, the pot assumed enormous proportions. But waking, she found the same day and night except that in the darkness it was more clear, the air smelled more heavily of the sewer in the canal, the carpets smelled more of dust.

On the fifth floor Jutta awoke and feeling less tired, began to wash a blouse in the hand-basin.

The tea was so near the chipped brim that it spilled over his robe when he peered closely at the cup and twisted it about. Stella drew the curtains but could see nothing, from the front windows neither street nor light, from the rear windows neither the line of the canal nor the shed. At first when the main pipes were destroyed she boiled the water that had to be taken from the canal, but for months the fire did not last long enough, the effort to prod the dull coals was too great, and tonight the tea tasted more sour than usual. In unlocking the basement door she had noticed that the smell of the canal was becoming stronger, the water seeping from its imperfect bed, and she decided that she must find a new place to keep the harmless unmoving man. The old woman, hair thin about her scalp but falling thickly to her waist, ankles frail without stockings in the high unbuttoned shoes, sipping tea through her thin once bowed lips, hated nothing, did not actually despise the gross invader or the struggling mistaken English, but would have been pleased to see them whipped. She knew the strength of women, and sometimes vaguely hoped that a time would come again when they could attack flesh with their husband's sickles, and the few husbands themselves could take the belts from their trousers to flay the enemy. It was the women who really fought. The uprising must be sure, and the place to strike with the tip of the whip's tail was between the legs. The candle went out and the brilliant old woman and crazed man sat in the darkness for a long while.

They had waited weeks for the riot to come at the institution and when it finally did descend like a mule to its haunches it lasted barely an hour. During those weeks disorder accumulated, both inside and outside the high walls. The German army was suffering unreasonable blows, the town was bereft of all men, the food trucks were overtaken by hordes of frenzied children, the staff itself worked in the gardens and nurses spent part of their duty in the bakery. Switchboard connections were crossed; Supply sent barrels of molasses but no meat; the cold came in dreadful waves. All reading material went to the furnaces; several cases of insulin went bad; and the board of directors learned of the deaths of their next of kin. Bedpans were left unemptied in the hallways; and for days on end the high bright gates of iron were never opened. Finally they burned linen for fuel and a thick smudge poured from the smokestack, the snow rose higher against the walls, and they served only one meal a day. One of the oldest night nurses died and her body was smuggled from the institution under cover of darkness. Reports crept out on the tongues of frightened help, of unshaven men, quarreling women, of patients who slept night after night fully dressed, of men who had hair so long that it hung on their shoulders. And those inside the walls heard that greater numbers of the more fit women were being taken to war, that there wasn't a single man left in the town, that Allied parachute rapists were to be sent on the village, that pregnant women went out of doors at night to freeze themselves to death.

The patients would no longer go to their rooms but crowded together in the long once immaculate corridors and baited each other or lay in sullen heaps, white with the cold. They had to be prodded into going out to the garden, white, filled with frozen thistle, and threatened, pushed, forced to retreat back to the buildings. Fearing more than ever erratic outbursts or startled, snarling attacks, the nurses quickly used up the last row of bottled sedatives, and old ferocious men lay only half-subdued, angrily awake through the long nights. One of these nurses, short, man-like, tense, lost the only set of keys that locked the windows shut, so for the last few days and nights, the horrible cold swept in and out of the long guarded wings. Underneath the ordered town-like group of brick buildings, there were magnificent tile and steel tunnels connecting them to underground laboratories, laundries, kitchens, and ventilated rooms that housed monkeys and rats for experimentation. Through these tunnels ran thin lines of gleaming rails where hand-carts of refuse, linen, chemicals, and food were pushed and the carts were guided by a meticulous system of red and yellow lights. During these bad days the carts were pushed too fast, knocked each other from the tracks, the system of lights smashed, the upturned carts blocked the corridors, and broken bottles and soiled linen filled the passages. The lighting system short-circuited and orderlies, now trying to carry the supplies in their arms, stumbled through the narrow darkness, through the odor of ferment, and shouted warning signals.

At last the rats and monkeys died. Their bodies were strewn over the main grounds, and since they froze, they looked life-like, tangled together on the snow.

All attempts at cure ceased. The bearded, heartening groups of doctors on rounds no longer appeared, nothing was written on charts. The tubs were left cold and dry, and patients no longer came back to the wards red, unconscious, shocked. Not only was treatment stopped, but all activity impossible. They no longer wove the useless rugs, no longer ran uncertainly about the gymnasium, no longer argued over cards or shot the billiard balls back and forth across the table. There were no showers, no baths, no interviews, no belts to make and take apart and make; and the news from the outside was dangerous. They could only be driven out to the garden and driven in.

Some insisted that the monkeys on the blanket of snow moved about during the night, and in the day it was difficult to keep the curious patients from the heaps of small black corpses.

The village, as the days grew worse, became a dump for abandoned supplies, long lines of petrol tins along the streets, heaps of soiled torn stretchers and cases of defective prophylactics piled about doorways, thrown into cellars. Piles of worthless cow-pod Teller mines blocked the roads in places and a few looted armored cars still smelled of burned cloth and hair. Women nursed children as large as six years old, and infrequently some hurrying official, fat, drunk with fear, would come into the village of women and bring unreliable news of the dead. Wives did not know whether their husbands were dead, or simply taken prisoner, did not know whether they had been whipped on capture or stood against a wall and shot. Hatless children ran through the deepening snow and chased the few small birds still clinging to the stricken trees. On the day before the riot an American deserter was discovered in a barn and, untried, was burned to death. Several pockets of sewer gas exploded in the afternoon.

It snowed for nights on end, but every morning the monkeys appeared uncovered, exactly the same as the day they were tossed into the yard, wiry, misshapen, clutching in their hands and feet the dead rats. When vigilance became more and more impractical, all poisons, orange crystals of cyanide and colorless acids, were thrown into the incinerator, and with despondent precaution all sharp instruments were destroyed. They were disturbed; several unrecognized, unwashed doctors wandered without memory in the pack of patients and one young dietician thought she was the common-law wife of a fifty-nine-year-old hebephrenic. On the night before the uprising, thieves tore down the wooden sign inscribed with the haven word "asylum," burned it during the coldest dawn recorded, and the institution was no longer a retreat.

Before dawn on the morning of the riot, Madame Snow stood alone by candlelight in a back room where cordwood had been piled, holding a stolen chicken struggling lightly beneath her fingers. She did not see the four stone walls or the narrow open window, and standing in a faded gown with the uneven hem that was once for balls, the untied soiled kimono flapping against her legs, she looked into the frightful eyes of the chicken and did not feel the cold. Her bare feet were white, the toes covered with grains of sawdust. The door behind her was locked, tallow dripped from the gilt holder and the bird fluttered, tried to shake its wings from the firm grasp. The old woman's pulse beat slowly, more slowly, but steadily, and the narrow unseen window began to turn grey. The feathers, bitten with mange, trembled and breathed fearfully. The soft broken claws kicked at her wrist. For a moment the Kaiser's face, thin, depressed, stared in at the cell window, and then was gone, feeling his way over a land that was now strange to his touch. The old woman watched the fowl twisting its head, blinking the pink-lidded eyes, and carefully she straddled the convulsing neck with two fingers, tightened them across the mud-caked chest, and with the other hand seized the head that felt as if it were all bone and moving bits of scale. The pale yellow feet paddled silently backwards and forwards, slits breathed against her palm. Madame Snow clenched her fists and quickly flung them apart so that the fowl's head spurted across the room, hit the wall and fell into a heap of shavings, its beak clicking open and shut, eyes staring upwards at the growing light. She dropped the body with its torn neck and squeezed with fingermarks into a bucket of water, and stooping in the grey light, squinted, and plucked the feathers from the front of her kimono.

A few moments later the messenger, angry, half-asleep, pounded on the window of the front room and shouted, "Riot, riot up at the madhouse," and clattered off, banging on more doors, calling to startled women, distracted, wheezing.

By the time Stella reached the Mayor's, still in the kimono, hair flying, she found a great quarreling crowd of women already gathered. The Mayor, before taking control of the villagers asked to send aid, had girdled the red sash around his nightgowned stomach, and distrait but strong, he stood on the ice-covered steps passing out equipment and words of encouragement to the already violent hags.

"Ah, Madame Snow, Madame Snow," he called, "you will take command on the march and in the attack. I leave it all up to you." Outstretched hands clamored in his face.

"Did you hear?" he shouted.

"Yes, I heard."

When all of the women had shouldered the barrel-staves which he had distributed, and fastened the black puttees about their bare legs, they started off, Stella in the lead and running as fast as she could. Jutta was tickling the Census-Taker at the time and only heard of the trouble afterwards. Madame Snow's hands were still covered with the blood of the chicken, and back in the small room its beak was clamped open. When they reached the iron fence and the gates were thrown open, the women stopped short, silent, moved closer together, brandished the staves, and looked at the band of inmates huddled together on the other side of the heap of monkeys. One of the monkeys seemed to have grown, and frozen, was sitting upright on the bodies of the smaller beasts, tail coiled about his neck, dead eyes staring out through the gates, through the light of early morning as dim and calm as the moon. "Dark is life, dark, dark is death," he suddenly screamed as the women charged across the snow.

All was hushed that morning, and in a dark wing of building 41, Balamir lay waiting among his unsleeping brothers and wished that someone would let in the cat. The male nurse who had been on duty three days and nights sat dozing in the stiff-backed chair and Balamir could see the white lifeless watch with its hanging arms. Along the length of the corridor were the rows of small empty rooms, and the signal lights over the swinging doors were burned out. An old cleaning woman, stooped and bent with the hem of her grey skirt hiding her feet, shuffled from the upper end to the lower of the monastic hall, dragging a mop over the outstretched legs, mumbling to herself, "Now it's quite all right, you'll all be well soon, yes, you'd be surprised at all I've seen come and go." The feathers of the mop were dry and frozen.

From the windows of building 41 one could see the irregular white fields stretching off to patched acres of sparse forest land, the game field with its bars and benches heaped with snow. Sometimes dimly through the grillwork of adjacent buildings, an unrecognizable single figure passed back into the shadows. The cleaning woman fumbled with the key ring fastened by a thin brass chain around her waist and went through the smooth metal door and down the deserted stairs. Suddenly a little wiry man with small fragile hands and feet and a clay pipe clutched in his teeth, ran to the door and facing it, trembled with anger.

"Don't you ever say such a thing to me again, don't you dare say that, if I hear it again, if you dare speak to me I'll break your back, I'll break it and cripple you, so help me," he screamed.

The nurse awoke with a start, reached for his smoldering cigarette. "Here, Dotz," he called, "stop that yelling . . ." but quickly, before he could move, the whole hallway of men, stamping and crying, followed Dotz through the door and out into the fresh air. Once out, no one knew the way in, and already a few white coats were excited and gave chase.

From a fourth floor window the Director, wrapped in a camel's hair coat, watched the struggle until he saw the women, led by Stella, rush the ridiculous inmates; he drew the blinds and returned to his enormous files.

During that hour the monkeys were so underfoot that the patients were saved from worse injury by the clumsiness of the women who shouted and tore and pelted everything in sight. As these women in the midst of changing years ran to and fro beating, slashing, the stiff tails and hard outstretched arms and furry brittle paws smacked against black puttees and were trampled and broken in the onslaught. Several wooden shoes were left jammed in rows of teeth smashed open in distortion by the stamping feet. The barrel-staves broke on unfeeling shoulders, the rats' bodies were driven deeper into the snow.

"Here, you," suddenly cried the cleaning woman from the main doorway, "come back in here," and the troop of men disappeared, kicking the stained snow in violent flurries. Suddenly the deputized women found themselves alone and standing on the mutilated carcasses of little men, and with a pained outcry, they fled from the grounds. "You won't say it again?" said Dotz, but no one answered and they settled back to rest in silence. The sun came out high and bright at nine o'clock and lasted the whole day, striking from the tiles and bricks, melting the snow, and the Director finally issued an order for the burial of the animals.

Leevey was killed outright when his motorcycle crashed into the log. He was pitched forward and down into an empty stretch of concrete. The Sten-gun, helmet, and boots clattered a moment, canvas and cloth and leather tore and rubbed; then he lay quiet, goggles still over his eyes, pencil, pad, whistle and knife strewn ahead. The three of us quickly leaped upward over the embankment, crouched in the darkness a moment, and then eagerly went to work. I was the first to reach the motorcycle and I cut the ignition, guided it over the bank. We picked up Leevey and carried him down to his machine, lost none of his trinkets, then together rolled the log until it slid down the muddy slope and settled in silence in a shallow stream of silt.

"It's not smashed badly," said Fegelein and ran his fingers over the bent front rim, felt broken spokes brushing against his sleeve, felt that the tank was slightly caved-in and petrol covered his hand. "You'll be riding it in a month."

I put my ear to the thin chest but could hear

nothing, for Leevey had gone on to his native sons who sat by the thousands amid fields of gold, nodding their black curly heads, and there, under a sunshine just for them, he would never have to bear arms again. The night had reached its darkest and most silent hour, just before dawn comes. Still there were no stars, the mist grew more dense overhead and even the dogs no longer howled. My fingers brushed the stiffening wrist.

"Are you ready?" asked my comrade by the machine.

I felt closer, more quickly, pulled away the cuff of the jacket, tore as quietly as possible at the cloth over the wrist.

"What's the matter with you? What are you doing anyway?" The voice was close; Stumpfegle also drew closer to my side.

"Eh, what's up?" The hoarse whispers were sharp.

I pulled at the strap, carefully, faster, and finally spoke, "He's got a watch." I leaned closer to the corpse.

"Well, give it here, you can't keep it just like that . . ."

I brought the pistol dimly into sight again, shoved the watch into my pocket, "I'm the leader and don't forget it. It's only right that I have the watch. Take the sacks off the machine and leave them here. We'll share what we can find, but not the watch."

Fegelein was already back tinkering with the engine. I listened to the watch and heard its methodical beat and could see the intricate clean dials rotating in precise fractions. The tongue was now sucked firmly and definitely into the back of Leevey's throat and his knees had cracked upwards and grown rigid. "We had better get him out of here." We picked him up and with the motorman between us stepped into the shallow ooze of the stream and headed out beyond the wall of fog towards the center of the lowlands.

On the opposite side of the highway, hidden in the shadows of unoccupied low buildings and the high bare spire wet with dew, stood Herr Stintz fixing everything closely in his mind, holding the little girl tightly by the hand. The child crossed and uncrossed the cold white legs, watched the black shadows leaping about in the middle of the road. Then they were gone.

Jutta yawned, carried the damp blouse into the next room, and opening the rear window, hung it from a short piece of wire dangling from a rusty hook. For a moment she smelled the sour night air, heard the lapping of water, and then returned to the still warm bed to wait the morning.

The limping English ghosts made their way back to the tank and stood silently waiting for the light when they would have to climb again through the hatch and sit out the day in the inferno of the blackened Churchill.

The Duke, breathing heavily, slowly extended his arm, and as the boy moved, clamped the diamond ringed fingers over the light shoulder and breathed easier. Footsteps sounded in the upper part of the clay-smelling theater and the projector began to grind and hum, then stilled again.

Very cold, the Mayor crawled out of bed, went to his closet and taking an armful of coats and formal trousers, heaped them on the bed. But it was still cold.

Madame Snow lit the candle again and saw that the quilted man was sleeping, and hearing no sound, no one returning to the second floor apartment, she decided to get dressed and simply await the day. She began to tie up the long strands of white and gold hair, and reaching into a bulky wardrobe found herself a formless white chemise.

"My God, the fog is thick."

"We're almost there," I replied.

"Which way?"

"A little to the right, I think."

The formless white puddles of fog moved, shifted among the stunted trees, rose, fell, trailed away in the areas of sunken swampwood where once tense and cowed scouting parties had dared to walk into the bayonet on guard, or to walk on a trigger of a grenade that had blown up waist high. An axle of a gun carriage stuck up from the mud like a log, a British helmet, rusted, old, hung by a threadbare strap from a broken branch.

"He's heavy."

"They feed the Americans well, you know," I answered.

"Well, he's going where they all belong."

Several times we stopped to rest, sitting the body upright in the silt that rose over his waist. A shred of cloth was caught about a dead trunk, the fog dampened our skin. Each time we stopped, the white air moved more than ever in and out of the low trees, bearing with it an overpowering odor, the odor of the ones who had eaten well. More of the trees were shattered and we, the pallbearers, stumbled with each step over half-buried pieces of steel.

"Let's leave him here."

"You know we cannot. Follow the plan."

Past the next tree, past the next stone of a gun

breech blasted open like a mushroom, we saw a boot, half a wall, and just beyond, the swamp was filled with bodies that slowly appeared one by one from the black foliage, from the mud, from behind a broken wheel. A slight skirmish had developed here and when the flare had risen over this precise spot, glowed red and died in the sky, some twenty or thirty dead men were left, and they never disappeared. The fog passed over them most thickly here, in relentless circles, and since it was easier to breathe closer to the mud, we stooped and dragged the body forward.

"You see, no one could ever find him among these. No one would ever look for him here." My idea for disposing of the body was excellent.

After searching the body once more, we left it and found our way again to the roadside. We took the machine and its valuable saddlebags silently through the town to the newspaper office.

"It's time we had our meeting," I said, "I'll be back." Fegelein began to work on the engine; Stumpfegle broke the head from a bottle.

The slut slept alone in her own house.

LAND

Madame Stella Snow's son, awakened by the barking of a dog, lay quiet, holding his breath like a child in the darkness. But it was not the dog that woke him, it was a theatrical sound, some slight effect, some trick of the playhouse itself, and he listened. Perhaps he had left the projector switch on, perhaps the lights were burning, or the spools of film unrolling. Whatever had happened, he did hear, in the intervals of distant howling, a woman's voice, an argument in the floors below between the empty seats. The dampness of the auditorium swept through the building, warehouse of old scenes, and his own bedroom, once a storeroom and place where the usherettes changed from frocks to uniforms, was cold and dark. It still smelled faintly of powder, stacks of mildewed tickets, cans of film and tins of oil. The voice, high and aristocratic, sounded like his mother's, changed, then seemed once more familiar. The girls had actually changed their clothes, changed into pants, in this room. The concrete walls, like a *bunker,* were damp and cold; light sockets, wire, and a few tools still littered the floor. The voices were still below, he thought he could hear someone weeping, the woman scolded, laughed, and talked on. His wife slept, her body shapeless and turned away under the quilt.

It took all of his effort to get out of the bed.

First, with one hand, he reached to the side and clutched the pipe that ran, cold to his fingers, under the mattress. With the other hand, he threw off the covers, and with a quick odd motion tossed his stump over the other leg, twisted his torso, flung his arm out to add weight to the stump's momentum, and precariously threw himself upright. It was even harder to get into the trousers; he succeeded by rocking forwards and backwards, pulling quickly with his hands, always with the good leg in the air keeping the balance. He smelled the perfume and old celluloid. Fixing his hands into the two aluminum canes, like shafts into a socket, ball bearings in oil, he made his way out into the hall, and since he couldn't as yet manage the stairs, hooked the canes to his belt, sat down, and holding the stump out of the way, made his trip bouncing down the three flights.

He could no longer hear the voices or the dog, only his own thumping on the cold stairs and the rattle of the thin metal legs dragging behind him. He moved like a duck, propelled himself forward with his two arms in unison and landed on the next step on the end of his spine. Something compelled him to move faster and faster until he was numb and perspiring, dropped with only the edge of the wall against his shoulder to guide him, fell with his palms becoming red and sore. Using the canes as props and the wall against his back he rose, laboriously, at the bottom of his flight, and listened for the woman's voice. But the voices had heard him coming, thumping, and were still. He waited, sensing them on the other side of the metal, fireproof door. He hesitated, then with an effort swung open the door and stepped into the rear of the auditorium, feeling in the dark many eyes turned upon his entrance. Slowly he hobbled forward, and seeing the large hat and magnificent cane, he laughed at himself and recognized the tall man.

"Ah, Herr Duke," he said, "I thought I heard voices in my theater. But did not expect this pleasure."

"You are right," said the Duke. "I've come after my neighbor's child, this boy here."

Then he saw the boy crouching down in an aisle, no longer weeping, but watching the two men. What a peculiar voice the Duke had, certainly a strange one considering his size and bearing.

"Boy, you should be home in bed."

"Yes," said the Duke in now more normal tones, "I'm taking him home. Forgive us the disturbance."

The child made no sound but allowed himself to be caught, in one quick swoop, about the wrist and pulled to his feet.

"Good night," said the tall man and left with his prize.

"*Ja, ja,* Herr Duke." The lame man watched the two go out into the still-wet streets, and turning himself, went back to the heavy door.

At the foot of the door his shoe was caught in a large poster, and looking down he saw an actress in a shining gown, wrinkled and scuffed about the breasts and hips.

"Good night, Herr Duke," he said, and freeing his single shoe from the woman's hold, he set out to climb back up the stairs. It was painful to his good leg going up, but even so he felt an uncommon pleasure in the visit of the Duke and the night's events.

I had been gone from the newspaper office only a moment, when Stumpfegle, who was drinking from the broken bottle, and Fegelein, who was rummaging through the motorcycle saddlebags, heard my footsteps returning to the door, and became alert. Both men looked up as I, their leader, stepped back into the office. I was hurried, disturbed, absorbed in the underworld of the new movement, bearing alone the responsibilities of the last attempt. I looked at my confederates and was annoyed with the liquor trickling from one chin, the contents of the bags strewn over the floor from the other's hands.

"Somebody saw us take care of the fellow on the motorbike."

"But, my God, Leader, what can we do?" Fegelein dropped a packet of Leevey's letters from him and looked up in fear.

"We'll have to change things. Bring the machinery, the arms, and everything else, to Command Two."

"Command Two?"

"Snow, idiot, behind Snow's boarding house."

Fegelein had the memory of a frog, a despicable blind green wart to whom all pads, all words, were the same.

"Bring the small press, the motor, bring all the materials for the pamphlets. Oh, yes, bring the whitewash."

"Leader, the machine will be ready to ride tomorrow . . ."

"Stumpfegle, you might ride yourself into the canal with ten American bullets, fired by well-armed Jewish slugs, in your fat belly, you childish fat fool. Don't *think,* do you understand, don't *think* of the machine, think of nothing except what we must do now. The night's not over, fat Stump-fegle, I don't want you shot. There are many *Anglo-Schmutzigs* we've got to poison with our print tonight. So please, just do the work." I nodded, forgot my temper, and slipped back into the darkness. Fegelein began to read the letters.

The oil flickered in the lamp, consumed and consuming, and as it burned, a few hoarded drops in the bottom of the tin, it shrouded the glass and beneath the film the flame was dimmed. After a considerable swig, the bottle, its neck jagged, filled and refilled, was put down on the floor, the dead man's letters were cast aside, unfit for reading, and the scraps, bundles, clips and type were collected. The patriots, fool and tinker, got themselves to work for power. It was no drunken lark. A difficult hour they had of it at that time of night, the worst time of night for odds and ends and order, especially after killing a man and with sleep so near. The light bright, the shutters drawn, the secret hard for dull minds to keep, the arms scattered, the work small and heavy, the very hardest time of night; this was the hour to try the henchmen.

In an alley by the press was a heavy cart, and Fegelein, the quicker of the two, made hurried trips with spools of thread, staples, needles, small loads of paper, and old bottles of ink. He thought of the witness and the accusing finger, saw the jurystand and unpredictable black-robed judge. Each time he dropped his load, so light but necessary, into the bottom of the cart, he looked up at the sky and feared the exposing dawn. There was no one to trust. Inside the shop the cobwebs were thick between the presses, the bottles piled higher near the rolltop desk, and old broken headlines were scattered, mere metal words, about the floor.

Stumpfegle, fat and cold, carried the small press out to the cart and rested. He carried the stitching machine out to the cart and waited, back by the lamp, for his friend to finish. Stumpfegle, ex-orderly and seeking power, torturer and next in command, harbored, beneath his ruthless slowness, the memory and the valor of his near suicide. Months before, he had lost his chance, though a better man than Fegelein. Stumpfegle, forty-two, aggressive, a private, was captured by a soldier from New York cited for bravery, when he wandered, dazed, into an American Intelligence Headquarters set up for propaganda work. Recognizing the *Reichsoldat,* the American immediately took Stumpfegle into the doctor's office, a room with a filing cabinet and fluoroscope. Quickly they put the big man under its watchful, scientific-research eye, and sure enough, imbedded far below his waist, between the sigmoid flexure and the end, they could see the silver object, the *Reichgeist* capsule, container of blissful death. An hour later, and while the soldier and the doctor watched, the purgative which they had given the bewildered prisoner worked, and Stumpfegle's last hope was dashed, in a moment of agony, down the privy-drain. He survived, with a soft pain where it had been, and gained his freedom to return to the new life.

"I'm finished except for the paint. We should hurry."

Stumpfegle slowly carried the can of whitewash to the cart, strapped himself between the heavy shafts, and with Fegelein wheeling the motorbike, they started down the dark street.

The Mayor fell asleep while vague white animals pranced and chattered through his dreams. Miller wished pain upon him, and kicked up his sharp heels and flew away, only to return with the Colonel on his back and a rifle under his belly to plague the poor mare, hot and sore with age. The white handkerchief was over his eyes, his legs were tied, and all those animals of youth and death, the historical beasts, danced about to watch. It was cold and the kitchen was empty.

The Duke and the boy were halfway down the hill towards the institution where a sack was hidden behind the town girls' bush. The dance music ceased in the storehouse below, the only lights were out. The cane once more was raised and the child, spattered with mud, tried without success to break away. A sleeper cocked his legs behind the storehouse.

"We're almost there. But let's try to hurry, will you?" The faster Fegelein tried to go, the more trouble he had with the machine. Yet he urged and he slipped. The shadow of the spy crossed their path.

The ghosts by the canal all watched, their heads together in the turret of the tank, the spirit of Leevey crawling to meet them from the dark water. A gaunt bird settled on the throat of the headless horse statue in the center of the town and mist fell on the grey sideless spire near the *Autobahn*.

The new watch on my wrist showed three o'clock. It was almost over. Tomorrow the loyal would know and be thankful, the disloyal would be taken care of. By tomorrow this first murder of the invaders would be public news; it would be, rather than a resistance, a show of strength. My footsteps echoed behind me in the darkness, somewhere the traitor was about, and then with a new energy swept upon me, I reached the boarding house. This town had no particular significance, as I entered the hall, because all towns were towns of the land, villages where idleness breeds faith, and the invaders hatred. Yet I knew this town, and in the days of power would always return, for I knew each disappointment, each girl, each silent doorway. I began to climb the stairs and on the next landing, knew the second floor boarder was still out.

My order, the new campaign, was planned and begun. It was spreading, conception and detail, to the borders of the land, aimed at success. The initial blow was struck, the enemy unseated, and there remained only the message to be dealt with and the traitor in our midsts to be undone. I opened the door and saw her warm and girlish arms.

It seemed she had been sleeping for only a moment and the bed was still warm where I had been.

The Census-Taker mumbled in his sleep two floors below, his shirt out of his trousers, wringing wet. They danced on his toes, it was so warm.

Gently pushing the covers back, she rolled slowly over, thinking of my warm brown chest.

Softly she spoke, "Come back to bed, Zizendorf." She wanted to fall asleep again.

She seemed to have forgotten, this flush Jutta, where I had been, love without sense. I sat in the chair facing the bed.

Then, curling her hair in her fingertips, stretching her knees, she remembered.

"It's done?"

"Of course. He fell as easy as a duck, that area-commander. He's out in the swamp with his comrades now."

"But how did you stop him?"

"The log." I bent over and loosened my shoes. "The log stopped him. You'd think that when he hit it he'd fly, perhaps swoop over it in a pleasant arc or at least in a graceful curve. But that's not true. He and the whole machine simply toppled over it, spokes and light and helmet flying every which way. Nothing grand about the commander's end at all!"

"You're safe? And now you can come and get warm."

Jutta feared cold as once she had feared the Superior's sun.

"The rest of the plan is still to be done."

Stintz pushed the child ahead with loving hands and silently she crept up the stairs. "You mustn't tell anyone what you saw, the moon will be angry," and she was gone into the darkness.

"I'd like to stroke your lovely heart and your hair. But there's still work."

"And I suppose there'll be even more when you reach success?" She yawned.

"Night should be mine, always."

The child stole into the room, back with Mother, shivering in her thin gown for all the long tiring adventure. I, the Leader, smiled, and Jutta held out her hand across the hard pillows and cold top-cover.

"My darling child, where have you been?" Absently she touched the thin arm and it felt hard, frail.

"What a strange little girl," I thought. Something stirred below, more like the sound of night than human, perhaps the mechanical movement of the trees against the house.

"I saw a man with a light, racing along where no one ever goes any more."

Surely this was not the spy, the lean shadow I had seen for a moment. But she must know the traitor, perhaps was taken in his bob-cat steps and walked by his side.

"What was he doing?" I spoke quietly with a special voice for children, carried over from the days before the Allied crimes and war.

"He didn't do anything. Somebody put something in the road and he was killed. His light was smashed."

"How did you go to see the man? Did someone take you for a walk?"

Suddenly she was afraid. She recognized my voice perhaps.

"The moon did it. The moon's a terrible thing in the sky and will be angry if I tell you anything. He'd kill me too."

"You go to bed, go to sleep," said Jutta, and the child ran into the next room. But she didn't sleep, she waited, awake in the dark, to see what would happen.

The honest man is the traitor to the State. The man with the voice only for those above him, not for citizens, tells all and spreads evil. His honesty is a hopeless misgiving. He makes the way intangible and petty, he hampers determination.

Stintz, barely back in his room, stood by the window and raised the sash. Peering with excited eyes, he looked at the turning in the darkness where he had first seen the light of the victim and tense with anticipation he slowly looked across the dark town-site, to the spot, what a joy, where the victim fell.

What a pleasure it had been, he knew I was up to something, and the child, this was the perfect touch, to make her follow the father and murderer through the darkness! Oh, he knew it was I all right, animal-devil, who took the blood tonight, but his thrill was in the justice, not the crime, no one would accuse except himself. Soon he would hear the footsteps, soon he would be the judge and all the knowledge would come to bear, in the rope, on the father of the child. The sky, for Stintz, was clearing; he hoped, in the morning, to inform.

Her face was so flushed, overjoyed with night, that I disliked leaving.

"I'll be back soon," I said, and she turned the other way to go to sleep. I heard the rustling again in the room below.

Stintz expected the knock on the door and said, "Come," almost before he heard it.

"Zizendorf," he said without turning, "come here."

The tuba lay on the floor between the visitor and host, instrument of the doleful anthem, puckered to the school-teacher's thin lips, battered and dull with long, tremulous, midnight sobs. Stintz still looked out of the window, as if to look all night and talk in the morning, alive and gaping over the streets he could never help to smooth and make prosperous, laughing and useless, watching the scenes of other people's accidents and deeds.

"What do you see?" I picked up the tuba and stood by the black-frocked teacher's side. I hated the braying sounds of the horn.

"Look. It's out again. The moon's out from behind the cloud. Look at him, he sees everything,

Zizendorf. He watches the lonely travelers, he hangs heavy over demons, terrible and powerful. The just man."

The edges showed white and distant for a moment and then the moon was gone. So faint, just a patch of grey in an unpleasant sky, that most people would not have looked at it a second time. Only the pious, with an inward craving for communion, would bother to crane their necks and strain their souls. I noticed that Stintz's neck jutted far out of the window, the bony face held rigidly upwards. The musty smell of textbooks lingered on the black coat, his arms were paralyzed on the sill.

The moon, the moon who knows everything, seemed to me like the bell of the tuba, thick and dull, awkward in my hands.

"You like the moon, don't you, Stintz? It seems frail to me, weak and uncolorful, tonight. I wouldn't put my faith in it."

His room should have been filled with clammy little desks, with silent unpleasant children to make faces.

"See here, I don't think I like your tone, you yourself may not be out of its reach, you know. There's retribution for everyone in this country now, justice, and it doesn't roll along a road where it can be trapped. Someone always *knows,* you really can't get away with anything . . ."

I swung the tuba short. I should have preferred to have some distance and be able to swing it like a golf club. But even as it was, Stintz fell, and half-sitting against the wall, he still moved for a moment.

Two things were wrong; there was the lack of room and I had misjudged the instrument itself.

Somehow thinking of the tuba as squat, fat, thinking of it as a mallet I had expected it to behave like a mallet; to strike thoroughly and dull, to hit hard and flat. Instead it was the rim of the bell that caught the back of Stintz's head, and the power in my arms was misdirected, peculiarly unspent. I struck again and the mouthpiece flew from the neck and sang across the room. I was unnerved only for a moment and when finally out in the hall, thought I would have preferred a stout club. Stintz no longer moved.

Stumpfegle and Fegelein were already encamped in the chicken coop, in the shed where the Colonel's jeep had been. I could hear them working as I walked across the yard behind the boarding house, their slight scuffle barely audible above the trickling of the canal. The pink pants and the plank that served as workbench had been tossed out into the darkness, and the shed was almost ready for the composition and the printing of the word. However, the cart was still loaded. I was disturbed to think that the press was not yet set up.

It was a heavy job to clear away the coating of chicken debris. The walls were thickly covered with the white plaster-like formations, hard and brittle, the effort of so many hens, less and less as the grain became scarce, finally water, with nothing left but the envied heaps of better days. Here and there a pale feather was half sealed in the encrustation. It would wave slightly, without hope of flight, embedded in the fowl-coral reefs of the wooden walls. The odor of the birds was in the wood, not in their mess; secretly in the earthen floor, not in the feathers. It was strong and un-removable. Fegelein hacked with a rusty spike, Stumpfegle slowly with the dull edge of a hoe, their dark suits becoming slowly speckled with calcium white.

I stood in the open door, trying not to breathe, allergic to the must-filled air, brushing the feathers and white powder from my jacket. I remembered the white women and darkness of Paris.

"I got rid of the traitor."

"But, Leader, that's magnificent." The foreign arm of justice, with its conundrums, lynchings and impeccable homes, lifted from Fegelein's brow, and the hard chicken foam gave with greater ease.

"It's one less fool to worry about, at least. And by tomorrow, we will have our public, proclaimed and pledged, every single one of them incorporated by a mere word, a true effort, into a movement to save them. Put into the open, the fools are helpless."

"Ah, yes," said Fegelein.

Stumpfegle hated the shed so much that he had no time for our talk. The odor of the flown birds, the stench, seemed like the country to him, and he was meant for the city, the shop with machines. "Birds piddle so," he thought, "it's unhealthly and unreal except for the smell."

"Success is almost ours."

Finally the shed was almost clean, with only a few globs left, and after quickly whitewashing the walls, they brought in the press, the stapler, the rollers and the reams of cheap paper. The three of us were spattered with the wash, became luminous and tired. Stumpfegle stood by the delivery table, Fegelein by the feed table, while I, the Leader, the compositor, put the characters, the words of the new voice, into the stick. I wrote my message as I went, putting the letters into place with the tweezers, preparing my first message, creating on a stick the new word. The print fell into place, the engine sputtered, filling the shed with the fumes of stolen gasoline. I wrote, while my men waited by the press, and my message flared from the begrimed black type:

INDICTMENT OF THE ALLIED ANTAGONISTS, AND PROCLAMATION OF THE GERMAN LIBERATION:

English-speaking Peoples: Where are the four liberties of the Atlantic Charter? Where is liberty and humanity for the sake of which your government has sent you into this war? All this is nothing as long as your government has the possibility of ruling the mob, of sabotaging Peace by means of intrigues, and of being fed with a constant supply from the increasingly despairing masses—America, who has fostered you upon a bereaved world only turns her masses of industry against that world, the muzzles of her howitzers of insanity and greed against a continent that she herself contaminates.

While you have been haranguing and speculating in Democracy, while you have branded and crucified continental Europe with your ideologies, Germany has risen. We proclaim that in the midst of the rubble left in your path there exists an honorable national spirit, a spirit conducive to the unification of the world and poisonous to the capitalistic states. The rise of the German people and their reconstruction is no longer questionable—the land, the Teutonic land, gives birth to the strongest of races, the Teutonic race.

People of Germany: We joyfully announce that tonight the Third Allied Commander, overseer

176

of Germany, was killed. The Allies are no longer in power, but you, the Teutons, are once more in control of your futures, your civilization will once more rise. The blood that is in your veins is inevitable and strong. The enemy is gone, and in this hour of extermination of our natural foe we give thanks to you, your national spirit that has flown, at long last, from Western slavery.

We pay tribute to the soul of Cromwell of the first war, who, realizing the power of the Goths and forsaking his weakened England, instigated the Germanic Technological Revolution. It is on his inspiration that the East looms gloriously ahead, and on his creed that the Teuton hills and forests will design their Native Son.

From the ruins of Athens rise the spires of Berlin.

I put down the tweezers. Without a word, but quivering with excitement, Fegelein locked the stick in place and the press murmured louder. Stumpfegle watched unmoved as the sheets, hardly legible, began to fall, like feathers, on the delivery table. Actually, I had never seen Berlin.

Madame Snow heard the animals rummaging in the shed, heard the foreign clatter disturbing the night.

"Ah, poor creature," she said, looking at the sleeping Kaiser's son, "they've come for you again." But Balamir did not understand.

Madame Snow's son eased himself laboriously back into bed, very much awake and excited with the effort of climbing, one leg, part of a leg, straight ahead, pulling as if it knew the way back up the stairs. The actress's face, just as bright as an usherette's, sniffed and startled, a smile on her lips, in the darkness. He pulled the covers up over his undershirt, leaned the canes against the bed. His wife did not breathe heavily enough to disturb him. He remembered with fixed pleasure, that night in the shed behind the boarding house and the girl from out of town with braids, who was pretty as a picture. She lost her pants in the shed and left them when the old Madame called and they had to run. In the late night he thought it was delightful, a skirt without the pants beneath.

"I haven't felt this way," he thought, with the Duke and child in the back of his mind, "since that ambulance ride four weeks after losing the leg. It was the bouncing of the car then, the driver said. Tonight it must have been jumping up and down the stairs."

Leg or no leg she'd lose them again. The boy certainly deserved the cane.

"Can't you wake and talk?" His voice was high and unnatural.

THREE

Balamir awoke with the sound of the engine in his ears and the arms of the Queen Mother holding him close. He wore his inevitable black trousers and black boots, the uniform that made the crowd in the streets bow down before their Kaiser's son, the black dress of the first man of Germany. For a moment he thought he was in the basement, in the sealed *bunker,* for the plaster of the walls was damp. But the Queen's hands, cooled with the mountain snow, touched his shoulder and the royal room, he laughed to himself, could not be mistaken for the cellar where he was sheltered in the first days. She had taken him from hiding, had evidently held his enemies at bay. Tonight the cabinet was reformed, the royal house in state, and the crisis, for the nation, passed. The Queen Mother herself had sent the telegrams, the car would be waiting, and the Chancellor would arrive with reports of reconstruction.

Something kept Madame Snow awake and now the poor man himself, after his peaceful sleep, looked up at her with those spiritless eyes and the impossible happy smile. She felt that powerful forces were working in the night and despite the fact that his presence was an extra obligation, she was thankful for him now. Perhaps he was like a dog and would know if strangers were about, perhaps his condition would make him more susceptible than ordinary men to the odd noises of the night. Would he whine if a thief were at the window? Madame Snow hoped, covering his shoulders more with the robe, that he would make some sort of noise.

The Duke, standing alone on the hillside in the hour before dawn, drew his sword with a flourish. The bottoms of his trousers were wet and ripped with thorns. He had lost his hat. His legs ached with the weariness of the chase, the silk handkerchief was gone from his sleeve, he stumbled in the ruts as he went to work. It was a difficult task and for a moment he looked for the moon as he cut the brush from the fox and found he had cut it in half. Looking up, lips white and cold, he could barely see the top of the hill. Over the top and through the barbed-wire was the rough path home. He hacked and missed the joints, he made incisions and they were wrong as the point of the blade struck a button. The fox kicked back and he was horrified. He hated his clumsiness, detested himself for overlooking the bones. Men should be precise either in being humane and splinting the dog's leg or in being practical and cutting it off. He would have preferred to have a light and a glass-topped table, to follow the whole thing out on a chart, knowing which muscles to cut and which to tie. Even in the field they had maps and colored pins, ways were marked and methods approved. The blade slipped and stuck in the mud, while his fingers, growing thin and old, fumbled for a grip, and his ruffled cuffs and slender wrists became soiled and stained. He should have had a rubber apron like a photographer or chemist, he should have had short sharp blades instead of the impractical old sword cane. The whole business bothered him, now after three or four hours of running about the town in the darkness. For the Duke was an orderly man, not given to passion and since there was a 'von' in his name, he expected things to go by plan. But the odds of nature were against him, he began to dislike the slippery carcass. It took all his ingenuity to find, in the mess, the ears to take as trophy, to decide which were the parts with dietician's names and which to throw away. At one moment, concentrating his energies, he thought he was at the top of it, then found he was at the bottom, thought he had the heart in his hand, and the thing burst, evaporating from his fingers. He should have preferred to have his glasses, but they were at home—another mistake. It was necessary to struggle, first holding the pieces on his lap, then crouching above the pile, he had to pull, to poke, and he resented the dullness of the blade. The very fact that it was not a deer or a possum made the thing hard to skin, the fact that it was not a rabbit made it hard to dissect; its infernal humanness carried over even into death and made the carcass just as difficult as the human being had itself been. Every time a bone broke his prize became mangled, every piece that was lost in the mud made the whole thing defective, more imperfect in death. It annoyed the Duke to think that because of his lack of neatness the beast was purposely losing its value, determined to become useless instead of falling into quarters and parts with a definite fore and hind. It lost all semblance to meat or fowl, the paw seemed like the foot, the glove the same as the shoe, hock and wrist alike, bone or jelly, muscle or fat, cartilage or tongue, what could he do? He threw them all together, discarding what he thought to be bad, but never sure, angry with his lack of knowledge. He should have studied the thing out beforehand, he cursed himself for not having a phial for the blood, some sort of thermos or wine bottle perhaps. He set something aside in a clump of grass and went back to work. But before he could lift the blade, he dropped it in indecision and searched through the grass. The piece he found was larger, more ragged. Perhaps the other was valuable and sweet, this was not. Tufts of the red fur stuck to his palm, a part of the shirtsleeve caught on his fingers. He wished for a light, a violent white globe in a polished steel shade, but this was the darkest part of the night. The task was interminable and not for a layman, and the English, he realized, never bothered to cut their foxes up. They at least didn't know as much as he. He sliced, for the last time, at a slender stripped tendon. It gave and slapped back, like elastic, against his hand. It would be pleasant, he thought, to pack these tidbits, be done with them, on ice. Someday, he told himself, he'd have to go through a manual and see exactly how the thing should have been done. The Duke put the blade back in its sheath and making a cane, he hooked the handle over his arm. The organs and mutilated pieces gathered up in the small black fox's jacket, he tied the ends together, used his cane as a staff, and trudged up the hill, his long Hapsburg legs working with excitement. Behind him he left a puddle of waste as if a cat had trapped a lost foraging crow. But the bones were not picked clean and a swarm of small cream-colored bugs trooped out from the ferns to settle over the kill.

I left Stumpfegle and Fegelein to distribute the leaflets. The sound of the press died out as I walked from the shed across the littered yard to the boarding house, the murmur of the canal grew louder with the rain from the hills that flowed, no crops to water, down into its contaminated channel. Somewhere near the end of the canal the body of Miller, caught under the axle of a submerged scout car, began to thaw and bloat.

Once more I climbed the dark stairs, deciding as I went, that in the weeks to come I'd turn the place into the National Headquarters. I'd use Stintz's rooms as the stenographic bureau, the secretaries would have to be young and blonde. I reached the third floor and a gust of cold wind, that only a few hours before had swept over the morning already broken in the conquered north, made me shiver and cough. My boots thumped on the wooden floor, my sharp face was determined, strained. It was a good idea, I thought, to make this old house the Headquarters, for I could keep Jutta right on the premises. Of course, the children would have to go. I'd fill the place with light and cut in a few new windows. That aristocrat on the second floor, the Duke, would perhaps make a good Chancellor, and of course, the Census-Taker could be Secretary of State. This town was due prosperity, perhaps I could build an open-air pavilion on the hill for the children. Of course I'd put the old horse statue back on its feet. Young couples would make love beneath it on summer nights. It might be better to mount it on blocks of stone, so that visitors drawing near the city could say, "Look, there's the statue of Germany, given by the new Leader to his country."

I pushed open the Census-Taker's door and by rough unfriendly shaking, roused my comrade out of a dead stupor.

"All the plans have been carried out. But there's something you must do."

I rubbed the man's cheeks, pushed the blue cap on more tightly and buttoned the grey shirt. I smiled with warmth on the unseeing half-shut eyes.

"Hurry, wake up now, the country's almost free."

After more pushing and cajoling, the old official was dragged to his feet, "What's the matter?"

"Nothing. Come with me."

"I'm too tired to sleep with that woman any more tonight."

I looked at him sharply. "We're not going to. Come along." I could not allow myself to be offended.

"I don't go on duty until eight o'clock."

I held my temper, for the old man was drunk and couldn't know what he was saying.

Together we climbed one more flight of stairs to Stintz's room, and pushing the tuba, with its little patch of dried blood, out of the way, we picked up the crouching body and started off with it.

"Nothing but water," said the Census-Taker struggling with the feet, "nothing but tuba and water and hot air out of his fat horn. Another pea in the fire of hell."

"Don't drop him."

"Don't drop him? I'd just as soon push him out of a window and let him get to the street by himself."

"We'll carry him, and you be careful."

The old man mumbled and pulled at the feet. "I won't even bother to take him off the roster."

Out in the street we propped the body against the stoop where the moon shone down on the upturned eyes and a hard hand lay against the cold stone.

"Go back to the paper, you know what to do. I'll meet you in front of the house." The Census-Taker, vice-ruler of the State, shuffled into the darkness and I went back to the shed to find the cart.

The Chancellery was still as cold as it was in its unresurrected days, and even at this hour the Chancellor, boarder of the second floor, was out. Madame Snow drew the curtains and found that it was still night, the smashed wall across the street was vague and covered with mist. Her loose hair hung in uneven lengths, where she had cut it, down her back, her face was white and old, pressed to the window. "If old Stintz wants to sit out there like a fool, well, let him. I'll make my imbecile some broth," she thought, and tried to stir up the stove but found it impossible. "You'll have to go without," she said to Balamir, and he started and grinned at the Queen Mother's words. Balamir knew that the village was like an abandoned honeycomb because somebody in airplanes had blown many of the roofs from the houses. But the Queen Mother should not look at the bleak night, it was his job and his alone to rebuild the town and make his subjects happy. He tried to attract her attention, but she was looking at the stove. Madame Snow herself wanted some broth, but collecting stove fuel from the basement was simply too great a task and she knew the fool, poor man, could never learn to do it. "Stintz is as bad as you," she said and crawled about the honeycomb chuckling to herself, tiara fallen to one side, grown loose.

Four flights up in my new rooms, the child got out of bed and once more stood by the window, beginning her vigil over the ageless, sexless night. The little girl, Selvaggia, was careful to keep her face in the shadow of the curtain, lest the undressed man in the sky look down and see. As much as she disliked Herr Stintz, she thought that someone should go and tell him to come back into the house. But she knew enough not to disturb her mother.

Jutta pulled the covers back over her shoulder. Now that I was gone, there was no need to expose herself to the cold, and even the Census-Taker was no longer interested in seeing. But she couldn't sleep. The peculiar thump of drunken feet, the droning of an engine, the footsteps of dead men echoed through the room, the branches scraped and whispered outside the window. She remembered the day that Stella went to be married and left her alone. Now Stella, the Madame, was old, only an old sterile tramp, and couldn't even keep the house quiet at night. Jutta drew her knee up, smoothed the sheets, and lay wide awake. She wished that I would hurry home. Men were so stupid about their affairs, running around with pistols, little short rods and worried brows. "Come to bed," she thought, "or one of these days I'll throw you out, Leader or not."

It was no use, there was no more sleep. She got out of bed and went to the three drawers under the washbowl stand and searched through her clothes. She found the letter under her week-day dress and it was covered with official seals and the censor's stamp. The letter from her husband before he was lost in Russia, imprisoned among Mongolians, was the only personal possession she had left. She held the paper up to the moonlight.

". . . I'm now at the front in a big field and the familiar world of men is gone. Yesterday a group went by and I shot the leader off his horse with a bullet right through his head. The rain sings and the streamlets reproduce every hour. I thought about him all last night and his horse ran off across the field. Now, Jutta, if it is true that I get what he used to own, I will send you the necessary papers so you can go and take possession of his farm. There may be a great deal of work to do on it so you had better start. I kept wondering last night if his wife was automatically mine or not. I suppose she is, and frankly, that worries me and I'm sorry I shot the fellow for that. I think she probably has red hair and the officials will dismiss the whole thing—but I will send you money as soon as it comes and you simply will have to make the best of it and fight it out with her and the children. His farm might be several acres, who knows? I'll send you maps, etc. plus the fellow's name and I don't think you'll have trouble crossing the field. I cannot make out what his wife will think of me now that she is mine along with the land. It's too bad for her that it had to be this way but perhaps there's a horse in the barn to replace the one that got away. I couldn't sleep at all because this field is in the open, which is most astounding, and I couldn't decide how much money he actually had that I could send you. I don't know how you feel about all this, perhaps you'll think I did wrong, but I struck the best bargain I could, and the Corporal in the dugout made it very difficult. Maybe I'll be able to end this slave rule and will certainly mend the roof on his farmhouse for you if you'll just do your share. There may be a few dogs on his farm who will keep the poachers off—I hope so. It's a terrible problem as you can see but if the Corporal comes on my side I think things will change. I hope the whole plan works out for you and the papers arrive safely through the rain, for at the same time I am doing nothing in the trenches and this excitement, over the wire and saddles, is disturbing my conscience . . ."

Jutta dropped the letter back into the washstand. She wished that it were a chest of drawers, a chest as tall as she and carved, with layer after layer of gowns and silk, something precious for every moment of the night, with a golden key and a gilded mirror on the top.

Stintz sat straight up in the cart, knocking heavily against the wood to the rhythm of the stones and fractures in the street. His face was set and he slipped, then righted, like a child in a carriage that is too large. He looked like a legless man hauled through the streets in the days of trouble, he was a passenger tensed for the trip with only his head rolling above the sides of the cart.

There was no straw in the bottom, his hands were locked rigidly apart, and he jiggled heavily when the wheels rolled over the gravel. If anyone else had been riding with him, he would not have spoken. He was surly, he was helpless, and his whole body had the defiant, unpleasant appearance that the helpless have. The shafts were too wide for me, and I had a difficult time pulling the cart, for sometimes it seemed to gather a momentum of its own and pushed me along while the heels behind me kicked up and down on the floorboards in a frightening step.

We met on the appointed corner and the Census-Taker put the tins, cold and unwieldly, into the cart. They quickly slid back into Stintz's lap, crowding him, pinning him down. He no longer slid with the movement of travel, he was no longer a passenger. The tins made the difference, they cut away his soul, filled the cart with the sloshing sound of liquid. His head was no longer a head, but a funnel in the top of a drum.

We stopped before the Mayor's door and struggled to get the martyr and the fuel out of the wagon. We dropped him and caught our breath.

"Are you sure he won't hear us?"

"He won't hear. And if he does, he won't do anything. I guarantee you he won't make a sound. He knows no one would help him."

With a great deal of effort, we dragged Stintz into the Mayor's hall and propped him against a table. We emptied the tins of petrol, ten *Pfennige* a cup, throughout the downstairs of the house.

It took a long time for the fire to reach the roof since the tins were diluted with water and the house was damp to begin with. The Census-Taker was forced to make several trips back to the newspaper office for more fuel and his arms and shoulders were sore with the work.

The Mayor thought that the nurse was preparing cups of hot broth and the kettle boiled as she stirred it with a wooden spoon. Little white pieces of chicken, whose head she flung in the corner, floated midway in the water. The warm fumes filled the room.

"Here, Miller," he said, "let's sit down to the soup together. That woman's an excellent cook and the bird's from my own flock. I have hundreds, you know. Miller, let me give you this broth." Tears were in the old man's eyes, he reached for the cup. But Miller wouldn't drink. The Mayor's nose and mouth were bound in the red bandanna, it choked about his throat, and at the last minute, Miller knocked over the tureen.

"I think we can go," I said. The fire was filling the street with a hot, small amount of ash.

The Mayor did not cry out, but died, I was very glad, without recompense or absolution.

The little girl had seen no fires since the Allied bombings, and in those days, she saw them only after they were well under way, after the walls had fallen and the houses did not look like houses at all. And the people crowding the streets after raids, running to and fro, giving orders, often made it hard to see.

Now, since the town had no fire apparatus, no whistles or trucks, and since there was no one in the streets, she could watch the fire as long as she wished; see it from her window undisturbed, alert. Firemen would certainly have destroyed the fire, their black ladders climbing all over the walls would have changed it, black slickers shining with water would have cried danger, covered with water they would have put it out.

The fire went well for a while, and then, because there was no wind to help it, no clothes or curtains to feed upon, it began to fade like an incendiary on the bare road, until only a few sparks and gusts of smoke trickled from the cracks of an upstairs shuttered window. The child soon tired of the flames that couldn't even singe a cat, but was still glad the fire-bell had not rung. She crept back under the covers to keep warm while waiting.

The Duke, his arms loaded with the shopping bag, wearily climbed the stairs and unlocked the door.

Madame Snow, hearing the noises overhead, knew that the second floor boarder was back.

The Signalman dozed in his chair and forgot the boy and the man with the upraised cane.

Madame Snow did not see the dying embers.

With his free hand the Duke put a few copies of the *Crooked Zeitung,* old unreadable issues, on a chair before resting his bundle; the white legs that dangled over the seat were too short to reach the rungs. A stain spread over the newspapers. He moved quickly about the majestic apartment, fit only for the eyes of a Duke, and now in his vest with his sleeves rolled up, he put two lumps of coal in the stove, rinsed his hands, and finally put the pieces in the bucket to soak. He put a few bones that he had been able to carry away, uninspected and unstamped, before the shop closed, on a closet shelf. After throwing the small fox's black jacket into a pile of salvaged clothes, he collected his pans and set to work. More newspapers over his knees, he gathered the pots about his feet and one by one he scoured, scoured until the papers were covered with a thick red dust, and the vessels gleamed, steel for the hearth. He scoured until his hands and arms were red.

The stove was crowded, for every pan and roaster that he owned was set to boil, lidded pots and baking tins, large and small, heavy and light, were all crammed together over the coals. The broth would last for weeks and months, his shelves would hold the bones for years. Through the shades a dull light began to fill the kitchen and at last, proudly, he was ready to go downstairs.

Madame Snow heard the footsteps, slow and even, stop before her door. She knew that something waited, that some slow-moving creature, large or thin, alive or dead, was just beyond, waiting to call. She heard the breathing, the interminable low sounds, the sounds so necessary to a nightmare, the rustling of cloth, perhaps a soft word mumbled to itself. If she turned on the light, he might disappear or *she might not recognize him,* she might never have seen that face, those eyes and hands, those rubber boots, and slicker drawn tightly up to the chin. It may swing an axe limply to and fro, large, ponderous, unknown. And if he did not speak but simply stood, hair wet over the eyes, face scarred, bandanna about the throat, and worse, if he did not move, never a step once inside the door with the white handkerchief, with the Christ by his head, with gauntlets and whistle that were never clutched, that never blew, on his belt, what would she do? She would not be able to speak, she would not recognize nor remember nor recall that peculiar way he stood, as if he held a gun, as if he had just climbed up from the canal with his slicker made of rubber rafts. She could hear him leaning closer against the door.

At last the knock came and cautiously and formally he entered.

"Ah, Herr Duke," she said, "good evening. You're visiting late, but it's a pleasure to see you."

He bowed, still in his vest, with arms red, and straightened stiffly.

"Madame Snow, I realize the hour, but," he

smiled slightly, "I have come on a most important mission."

She clutched the robe, the Queen Mother's before her, close to her chest.

"I would be most happy," continued the tall man, "if you would give me the pleasure of dining with me, full courses and wine, at ten o'clock this morning that is to come. I have been most fortunate, and the meal is now being prepared."

"It is an honor, Herr Duke."

With one more bow, sleeves still rolled, the Chancellor climbed the stairs. He was the bearer of good tidings.

Balamir was startled to see, only a few moments after the Chancellor took his leave, Madame Snow stoop to seize a piece of paper that had been thrust beneath the door. They heard the messenger, Fegelein, cantering off down the greying street, heard the slamming of several doors. Madame Snow squinted by the window, her long hair shaking with excitement. She read and disbelieved, then read again. This joy was too much to bear, too great, too proud. Tears of joy and long waiting ran down her cheeks, the pamphlet fluttered from her hands, she clutched at the sill. Suddenly, with the energy of her youth, she flung open the window and screamed towards the upper stories of the boarding house.

"Sister, Sister, the news has come, the liberation has arrived. Sister, thank your countrymen, the land is free, free of want, free to re-build, Sister, the news, it's truly here." She wept as she had never wept when a girl.

Only silence greeted her cries. Then the child called fearfully down, "Mother is asleep." A bright excited day was beginning to dawn and a few harassed and jubilant cries, no more, echoed up and down the drying streets.

Even though the print was smeared quite badly, and some of the pamphlets were unreadable, the decree spread quickly and most people, except the Station-Master who didn't see the white paper, heard the news and whispered about it in the early morning light, trying to understand this new salvation, readjusting themselves to the strange day. The decree was carried, faithfully, by Stumpfegle and Fegelein who walked in ever widening circles about the countryside. They walked farther and farther, growing tired, until even the spire, struck with sunlight, was no longer visible.

In Winter Death steals through the doorway searching for both young and old and plays for them in his court of law. But when Spring's men are beating their fingers on the cold earth and bringing the news, Death travels away and becomes only a passer-by. The two criers passed him on his way and were lost in an unbounded field.

The Census-Taker slept by the bottles in the newspaper office, his hands and face still grey with soot.

Madame Snow hummed while she tied up her hair.

Her son finally slept.

The hatches on the tank were closed.

The decree worked, was carried remarkably well, and before the day had begun the Nation was restored, its great operations and institutions were once more in order, the sun was frozen and clear. At precisely ten o'clock, when the Queen Mother went to dine, the dark man with the papers walked down the street and stopped at the boarding house. As Balamir left the castle with the shabby man, he heard the faraway scraping of knives and forks. At the top of the hill he saw the long lines that were already filing back into the institution, revived already with the public spirit. They started down the slope and passed, without noticing, the pool of trodden thistles where the carrion lay.

I was surprised to hear all the laughter on the second floor, but was too tired to stop and receive their gratitude. Beside the bed in Jutta's room I stripped off my shirt and trousers and with an effort eased myself under the sheets. I lay still for a moment and then touched her gently, until she opened her eyes. The lips that had waited all evening for a second kiss touched my own, and from the open window the sharp sun cut across the bed, shining on the whiteness of her face who was waking and on the whiteness of my face who had returned to doze. We shut our eyes against the sun.

Selvaggia opened the door and crept into the room. She looked more thin than ever in the light of day, wild-eyed from watching the night and the birth of the Nation.

"What's the matter, Mother? Has anything happened?"

I answered instead of Jutta, without looking up, and my voice was vague and harsh; "Nothing. Draw those blinds and go back to sleep . . ."

She did as she was told.

New Directions Paperbooks

* Paperbound over boards.   † Bilingual.
(SFR) A New Directions / San Francisco Review Book.

Complete descriptive catalog available free on request
from New Directions, 333 Sixth Ave., New York 10014.